Arena Beach

Donna Staples

Houghton Mifflin Company
Boston 1993

Library of Congress Cataloging-in-Publication Data

Staples, Donna.
    Arena Beach/by Donna Staples.
        p.   cm.
    Summary: Raised in an unconventional fashion by a former hippie
mother who now seems to be retreating from the real world, seventeen-
year-old Tee finds her life further confused by the sudden
appearance of the father she has never known.
    ISBN 0-395-65366-5
    [1. Fathers and daughters — Fiction.   2. Mothers and daughters —
Fiction.   3. California — Fiction.]   I. Title.
PZ7.S79344Ar   1993   92-36302
[Fic] — dc20   CIP
                             AC

Printed in the United States of America

AGM   10 9 8 7 6 5 4 3 2 1

For my family —
and all families —
wherever and whatever
they may be.

Chapter 1

The school bus barreled down the mountainside and exploded from the thick redwood canopy. The ocean flashed into view. Hazy sunlight glared slickly off the water. Itching to complete his run, the bus driver leaned hard into the next hairpin turn. The right rear wheels skidded off the pavement and bumped wildly along the narrow shoulder above a sheer, hundred-foot drop. The driver wrenched the steering wheel with both hands, slammed on the brakes, then punched the accelerator. Biting asphalt and spitting gravel, the bus lurched back onto the roadway and continued down the mountain toward the beach.

I hadn't ridden the bus in over a year. Since the day after I turned sixteen and got my license, I'd driven myself over the mountain to high school and back every day. Now my car was in the local garage with a leaky carburetor. If the new gasket had been delivered, which wasn't exactly guaranteed because UPS believed we lived in some provincial backwater hundreds of miles from civilization, I could install it that afternoon. If the gasket hadn't arrived, I'd skip school tomorrow.

No way would I voluntarily ride this instrument of death and degradation again. The vinyl seats smelled like rotten oranges and dirty socks and other things too disgusting to mention. I sat with my face out the window, trying desperately to keep my mind off the bus's lurching and swaying by thinking of something else. Like my boyfriend. And my mother. And what I might cook for dinner that night. But no matter how much I tried to divert my mind, it veered right back to the road.

I was thirteen the first time I negotiated the mountain highway myself. My mother, who didn't drive, had reserved a booth at an arts and crafts fair in Sausalito. The friend who had promised to transport her came down with a salmonella infection at the last minute and offered her his car. "You'll be better at this than I will, I'm sure," my mother said as she handed me the keys. "You've always been good with machines." Wearing a scarf and sunglasses so the sheriff wouldn't stop me for being underage, I motored over the mountain at about five miles an hour. By the time we reached the freeway, my shirt was soaked, my lower lip bloody and permanently imprinted with teeth marks. But I didn't go off the road once, unlike this stupid bus driver who drove like a maniac in a demolition derby.

We finally reached the outskirts of Arena Beach. The driver actually slowed down for the last sharp curve before careening toward downtown. We passed the volunteer fire station and the Dunes Motel, disturbed a few stray dogs napping in the shade of the Sand Bar's front porch, then slipped past the Lip, short for Off-the-Lip, the local surf shop.

Through the store and out the rear door, I caught a quick glimpse of my boyfriend, Skeg, stooped over the custom surfboard that had consumed most of his attention for a full week. He'd already air-brushed a wicked sea monster with a bloody human leg dangling from its jaws. Now he was filling in the details — a pack of sharks circling the mangled leg, snatching bits of flesh.

Soft-spoken and gentle, Skeg was the sweetest person I'd ever known. Often I wanted to reach out, scratch his head, and fluff his sun-bleached hair as if he were an orphaned cat, but usually I restrained myself. Touching him a little made me want to touch him more.

Although we'd known each other for over a year, Skeg and I had been going out for only a few months. One day when I went into the Lip to buy some number twenty-five sunscreen for my peeling nose, he quizzed me about his VW bus's overheating problems. I told him about the cylinder that always burns up on those surfmobiles. He asked me out.

Now, as I thought about his muscled back, viewed from the bus window, I reflected that I might be one of the few remaining virgins in the senior class of Sequoia High School. How much longer I'd hold out, given the way I was rapidly revising my previous, less-than-noble opinion of surfers, was anybody's guess.

Wheezing and coughing and smelling of burned rubber, the bus jolted to a halt at the stop sign in the center of town. I grabbed my backpack, hopped down the steps, and took a deep breath of salt air.

Arena Beach is sandwiched between a three-thousand-foot mountain and the Pacific Ocean. The town itself is no big deal — a few blocks of flimsy cottages, a handful of struggling businesses. Arena has no movie theater, no drugstore, no bank. Not even a traffic light. But the beach, a long clean curve of sand with spectacular waves, dazzles the senses. Born in Arena, I'd lived there all my life and couldn't imagine moving anywhere else.

As I crossed the dusty intersection toward the gas station, I noticed Pegasus reappearing again. Decades ago, the station was a Mobil franchise. When business took a dive during the oil crisis of the seventies, the former owner could no longer afford a name brand. He whitewashed over the flying red horse and became an independent dealer. Later he sold the business to my friend Turbo and moved to Santa Fe. Now, every

4

few years the persistent winged creature bled through, reminding all the locals that the station, and the town, had once been more prosperous.

I kicked one of the work boots sticking out from beneath a newish silver Toyota pickup.

"Hey, Tee," a deep voice grunted from under the truck.

"Hey, Turbo. How's it going? My gasket come in yet?"

"What's a nice girl like you want with a new gasket? It's too ugly for jewelry, and it sure won't keep you from getting knocked up, no matter where you wear it." The rest of him appeared suddenly on the oil-stained pavement. He was so big he completely smothered the dolly beneath him. Neckless, his jowls running from his cheeks to his shoulders and into a greasy T-shirt, he looked like one of the large harbor seals that sunbathe on Pickleweed Island at low tide. Rolls of blubber rearranged themselves as he raised his head and winked at me.

I locked wrists with him, planted my shoes firmly on the cement, and hoisted his huge bulk off the dolly. "Your mind's as dirty as your hands," I said, turning away so he wouldn't see the red flush uniting all the freckles on my cheeks.

Turbo enjoyed playing the role of a jolly, dirty old man, a cross between Santa Claus and W. C. Fields. Most of his jokes were stupid or gross or both. Despite his sick brain, I liked him.

Turbo's age was a mystery. Maybe his fat camouflaged age wrinkles. The way he dressed, in farmer overalls and T-shirts, provided no clues. He could have been anywhere from thirty-five to fifty-five. He was definitely old enough to be my father.

I used to wonder what it would be like to have a dad like Turbo. Not too many fathers drove Harleys or listened to heavy metal. Turbo was a good teacher, softening his sarcasm with patience when I couldn't tell the difference between a tick and a knock, a hot wire and a dead one. But he was pigheaded about running things his own way. And he certainly didn't set a good example of how to take care of yourself. He smoked a couple packs of cigarettes a day and took in more cholesterol than a starving tourist at a luau. No, he wouldn't have made a good father, I'd decided. But then, what did I know about fathers?

A driver pulled up to the pumps in a big brown Caddie with an Avis sticker on the bumper. "Your, uh, gasket is on the desk, ma'am," Turbo said with a lewd wink as he shuffled over to the Cadillac, swinging each leg around the bulk of the opposite thigh.

The office reeked. Turbo's desk was littered with old engine parts and invoices, half-empty cans of transmission and brake fluid, slimy Styrofoam cups and moldy bits of food, ashtrays overflowing with butts, mostly Kool 100s. A thick layer of scum and dust coated the desk's metal surface.

When I first started working for him, I'd been so

disgusted by Turbo's mess that I came in early one Saturday to tidy up. As the sun rose and struggled through the filthy windows, I transferred cans to a shelf in the shop, tossed cups and food scraps into a dumpster outside, emptied ashtrays. Suddenly the room turned dark. Turbo, his face twisted and flushed, blocked the doorway. "Keep your prissy little nose out of my business," he spat slowly through his fat jowls.

Later he brought me a cup of hot chocolate from the Snack Shack and apologized. He told me about his mother, an obsessively compulsive woman who'd made his childhood miserable. She'd forced him to clean every bit of food off his plate at every meal and fined him a quarter for each piece of clothing she found on the floor of his room. When Turbo graduated from high school, he moved out of her squeaky clean house and got a job at a truck stop repairing big rigs. He vowed he'd never again let anyone tell him what to eat or how to clean up his room. Or his office.

I spotted my gasket on top of a pile of dirty air filters on Turbo's desk, then located the top half of my carburetor on the messy workbench in the shop. Leaning against the bench, I began to peel off the old gasket while I surveyed my baby — a 1964 Buick Skylark sedan.

I called her the Gray Whale. Rust patches bubbled through the old paint like barnacles on a whale's flukes. She wasn't fancy. Just good, solid Detroit iron, as Turbo had said at least once a week since he first helped me get her running. In the sixties, people called the Skylark a compact, but she actually outsized the new Cadillac pulling away from the pumps. Skeg's surfboard fit easily in her trunk.

My mother bought the car for me a few months before I turned sixteen. She needed a chauffeur and I needed a sane alternative to the school bus. When she found this "mechanic's special" advertised in the local rag, she talked Turbo into advising me. He gave me a job at the station, then gave me lessons in auto repair during the slow hours. The Whale provided lots of hands-on experience. After we'd completely overhauled her, Turbo let me stay on at the station part-time. He couldn't afford to pay me much, but the fringe benefits — free advice on everything from cam shafts to condoms — were invaluable.

"Hey, Turbo," I yelled out the open doors, "where'd you hide the sealant?"

He waddled around the corner and squeezed between the Whale and the cluttered bench. "Right beside your carburetor, genius." I looked over the mess again and, sure enough, spotted a wrinkled tube of gasket sealant half hidden by a length of rubber radiator hose. "I thought you were learning how to make accurate observations in those soul-stirring science classes of yours."

"This," I said, sweeping my hand over the surrounding clutter, "is no science lab."

He took the carburetor from my hand, drew a small jackknife from his overalls, and began scraping off the last remnants of old gasket and sealant.

"Your mother home today?" he asked as I loosened the cover from the metal tube with my teeth.

"I guess. She had some people coming in for sessions. Why?"

"The jackass in the Caddie asked if I knew her. Told him I recognized the name. Figured he could look up your phone number and get directions from your mother if she wants to see him."

"Great. Another yuppie customer. What do you think this one will pay her?" I spread a layer of sealant on the bottom half of the carb with my finger.

"I suppose that depends on what she does for him. Doesn't she usually ask her clients to pay what they think she's worth? Easy now. Put on too much and that thing'll slide around like bald tires on an oil slick."

I wiped a glob of sealant off the block and carefully set the new gasket in place. Then, just as I was lining up the holes on the top half of the carburetor with the holes on the gasket, I felt something brush against my hair.

"What're ya doin', Tee?" Skeg whispered in my ear.

Skeg never appreciated how much concentration was required to fit parts together properly. Maybe it was his artistic temperament, his right brain tenden-

9

cies. In any case, he didn't know a thing about cars. While he danced his fingers on my spine, I gritted my teeth and settled the carb on the new gasket. Then I straightened up and moved back from the Whale so nothing would get bumped accidentally. What did he think I was doing — brushing my teeth?

"I'm fixing my car." I looked into his gray-green eyes, tide pools on a cloudy day, then looked away quickly. "What are you doing?"

"Checkin' the waves." When he grinned, his teeth flashed white against his bronzed skin. The top half of his wetsuit hung around his hips. I swallowed, wanting to touch his bare chest, but Turbo lurked nearby. Besides, there was too much daylight for any display of affection. Or lust. "Want to come?" he asked. I watched his lips form the words.

Turbo leered at me across the engine. I ignored him.

"Can't. I've got to finish this for tomorrow."

"Oh, I must go to school tomorrow," Turbo said in a high, mincing voice. "I'm such a good girl. I never do anything bad."

Right then I wanted to strangle that thick neck of his. Why did he always give me such a hard time? "Butt out, Turbo."

"Difficult, with a butt this size, but not impossible. Say please."

Skeg slid silently out of the shop, grinning lopsidedly, avoiding Turbo's poisonous tongue the way he'd skirt a Portuguese man-of-war. "Are you eating dinner with us tonight?'' I called after him as he tucked his board under his arm.

I thought I saw him nod before he turned the corner.

Turbo fished a crumpled pack of Kools from the bib of his overalls. He knocked the pack against his thick forearm and pulled out a mashed cigarette.

"I don't want to hear a word about the goddamn surgeon general,'' he growled when I made a face at him. He walked over to the doorway and glared up and down the empty street while I hunted for a small standard screwdriver.

I used to wonder if Turbo had a death wish. It wasn't just the cigarettes. He refused to wear a motorcycle helmet, claimed they were all too tight for him and blocked his vision. And he drank far too much. One of these days he'd have an accident or blow up the entire garage with his smokes. I only hoped I'd be out of town when it happened.

Turbo flicked his cigarette stub into the bushes in the vacant lot next door. "So what did you cover today in physics, genius?'' he asked, coming back inside to help me hook up my hose lines and linkage.

Turbo and I spent a great deal of time between customers discussing my studies. When I first started working for him, I simplified my classroom lessons into what I figured a competent automobile mechanic might comprehend. Then my mother told me about Turbo's doctorate in astrophysics from Stanford.

11

When I accused him of deliberate deception, he just asked me to explain that bit about falling objects again.

I am definitely not the intellectual type. In school I secretly enjoyed algebra and geometry — all those equations and proofs, everything making sense, coming out balanced. And I found physics reasonably interesting — sound waves and levers and pulleys. Practical stuff. But I felt extremely uneasy with things like mesons and quarks, quantum logic and the two-fold reality of potentials. What did Heisenberg mean by *probable* reality? I preferred Descartes' mechanistic world view and Newton's Third Law of Motion — for every action there is an equal and opposite reaction.

Nearly everyone in my class at Sequoia planned to go on to college. They'd all sent off stacks of applications and now, in April, raced home after school every day to check their mail. A thin envelope meant a rejection, fat for acceptance. One kid in last year's graduating class almost died of an overdose of aspirin when he received skinny envelopes from Harvard, Duke, and UCLA on the same day.

I didn't need that kind of stress any more than I needed a college degree. Skeg had never even finished high school and he managed the Lip as well as any college graduate. Turbo said that college would be a waste of time if I didn't know what I wanted to do with my life. (Maybe even if I did know.) My mother believed that education was never wasted, but she didn't try

12

to influence my decision. The guidance counselor at school was another story. He thought I wouldn't be living up to my potential if I stayed in Arena and worked for Turbo. He kept reminding me that the local junior college accepted applications into July. I still had time to change my mind.

I pumped the accelerator to get some gas into the carb, then turned the key in the Whale's ignition. The engine turned over and caught. I hopped out to check for leaks.

See, I reassured myself, *I am a good mechanic. I don't need a college degree. I'm not interested in any high-status, high-paying job. I already live in a beautiful place. I'm not supporting a cocaine habit. I don't drink and I wouldn't be caught dead in a designer dress. I like working on cars because, when something goes wrong, there's always a reason. You find the problem and fix it. Simple. What more could I learn in college that would help me get through life?*

The sun hung low on the horizon when I eased the Whale into our driveway. I listened happily to the engine for a minute, then turned the key. I dragged a bag of groceries across the front seat, looped my backpack over one shoulder, and closed the car door with my hip.

Just then I noticed a brown Cadillac parked in the shadows up the street. The man who'd asked Turbo about my mother sat behind the wheel watching the ocean — or me — through a pair of binoculars. I shook my head and went inside.

"Hi! Celestial?" The living room of our tiny cottage was empty, but I could hear water running in the bathroom. I set the bag of groceries on the kitchen counter, walked back through the living room, and knocked on the bathroom door.

"I'm home."

"Hello, darling. Come in so I can hear you better." I cracked open the door. A warm rush of musk-scented steam filled my nostrils. "Did you have a good day, Tee? What happened with your French quiz? How's the Whale?" My mother often spoke in a series of questions. Usually I just answered the last question in a line-up, figuring the others would turn up sooner or later at the end of another spiel.

"All fixed. How was your day?"

"Busy. I'm exhausted. Three clients this afternoon, each in a separate session. It's much less tiring when they agree to work in groups. And I focus my energies better that way. But these three were all concerned about privacy." I scraped the grease from my thumbnail with a machine screw I discovered in my back pocket. I didn't like to discuss her work. "How's Turbo? Did you talk to Skeg? What about your homework? Do you want to fix dinner, or shall I?"

"I'll cook." If I didn't we'd probably have cottage cheese and fruit or peanut butter sandwiches or tofu with sprouts. A vegetarian, my mother was not exactly what you'd call overly ambitious in the kitchen. And while my favorite item on the Snack Shack's menu was a double bacon burger with a side of fries, at home I stuck to grains and veggies and dairy products. "I picked up an eggplant at the store. How's about a little *parmigiano, Mama mia?*"

"*Perfètto, mia bambina.*"

"No need to rush your bath. It'll take a while."

"Thanks, darling."

I cut the eggplant, salted the slices, and spread them over several thicknesses of paper toweling. While the moisture soaked into the towels, I crumbled some crackers and scrambled two eggs with a splash of water. Over my shoulder, through the large living room window, I could see the ocean turning a deep cobalt blue, the sky tangerine. A large container ship was silhouetted against the orange sky.

As I dipped the eggplant slices first in seasoned flour, then in egg, and finally in the cracker crumbs, I studied the freckles on the back of my hand. My mother's skin was rosy-beige and clear. I wondered whether someone in my father's family had the same pale, freckled skin as mine. Or burned as easily. One reason I never learned to surf was that I couldn't stay in the sun without turning into a boiled lobster. (The other reasons were sharks, cold water, sharks, undertow, and sharks, in that order.) The eggplant sizzled when it hit the hot olive oil in the skillet. I layered the

15

browned slices with tomato sauce and mozzarella in a casserole dish. That was an awfully big blotch on the back of my left hand. Cancer? Irregular edges was one of the danger signs, and this looked like a miniature map of France.

I popped the casserole in the oven, grabbed a Coke, and plunked down in the old wingback chair in the living room. The freighter, its lights standing out clearly now against the inky water, moved deliberately toward the Gate. I sank back in the chair and watched a few rabid surfers still taking advantage of the evening glass-off.

Skeg surfed almost as well as he painted but didn't make enough money at it to support himself. This was his second year on the U.S. Pro Tour. I'd never seen him compete and wasn't sure I wanted to — all those girls hanging all over him at the competitions. Besides, the events this year had been too far away — Puerto Rico, Hawaii, North Carolina. Maybe I'd watch him in Santa Cruz in May.

Skeg grew up in Baltimore, Maryland, a hundred miles from the Atlantic Ocean. Every summer his whole family — Skeg and his four older brothers and their parents — spent a week at the shore. The waves at Ocean City weren't very good, and the water was sometimes filled with jellyfish that left red welts on your skin if you touched them. But Skeg had been hooked the first time he caught a ride on a longboard there.

The summer Skeg's brother Theodore graduated from high school, the two of them hitchhiked to Southern California in search of the perfect wave. At the end of August, Theodore went back to Baltimore and started working for Domino Sugar, but Skeg stayed in California. He hadn't been back to visit in five years, had never met his brother Franklin's wife, or seen Woodrow's twin daughters. His mother wrote to him on the first day of each month, filling him in on Woodrow's double hernia operation and the twins' teething progress. And he called her around the middle of each month to ask what his father was doing with his retirement, how she was faring with the old man around the house all day, how Calvin liked his new job, if Franklin's wife had come back to him yet.

I learned most of the tidbits about his family by eavesdropping on the telephone calls to his mother. He phoned her from the Lip, where he lived in a loft above the store, and talked to her while I stayed downstairs and put the bikinis in order or swept the sand off the floor. "Hello, Ma? It's me. Harry," he shouted into the receiver. His mother had a hearing problem. "How ya doin', Ma?"

I raised the Coke can to my mouth. Empty. The freighter had disappeared, the surfers given up the waves. The eggplant would be done soon. I glanced at my watch but couldn't read the dial in the dim light.

A car headed up the street. Skeg? No, that was no

Volkswagen engine. That brown Cadillac again. I listened to it motor past the house. The driver might be some kind of weirdo scoping out my mother's business. A prospective customer or an IRS agent? I couldn't decide which would be worse.

Celestial padded barefoot into the living room and switched on a lamp. She wore a purple bath towel turban-style over her hair and a red silk kimono embroidered with flowers and butterflies. "Why are you sitting here in the dark, darling? The eggplant smells divine. Is Skeg coming for dinner? Have you seen Mao since you got home? I'm afraid the raccoons chased him away again. Shall I make a salad to go with the casserole?"

Chapter 2

The window on the driver's side of the brown Cadillac slid silently down. Turbo was taking a break, so I walked over to the car to see what this character wanted.

"Hi," he said, a stiff, fake smile on his lips. Who did he think he was fooling? "Would you fill it with supreme?"

He handed me his keys. I unlocked his gas cap and jammed the hose nozzle into the tank opening. When I tossed the keys back, he missed and had to bend over to retrieve them from the floor. Klutz.

I grabbed a squeegee from the bucket beside the pump. Washing his windshield gave me a chance to check him out. He wore a pink button-down collar shirt, the sleeves rolled up almost to his elbows. His skin was pink, too. He'd probably spent too many hours on the beach without sunscreen. His forehead was bald. He whistled an old Beatles tune and tapped his fingers on the leather-covered wheel. I could see a California road map and a large pair of binoculars on the passenger's seat. Was he a bird watcher or a peeping Tom? He wore a gold band on his left ring finger, but the worst perverts, I knew from the newspapers in the grocery store, were married.

I flicked the water off the squeegee. "That'll be three seventy-eight."

"I guess it wasn't as low as I thought. Always good to have a full tank out here in the boonies, though. Right?" He handed me a twenty.

"Just passing through?" I asked casually as I gave him his change.

"Not exactly." He nodded toward the motel. "Does every town on the coast have a place called The Dunes?"

"Or a Sandpiper, Spindrift, or Seaside. California Coastal Commission Regulation Seven sixty-one."

"That's a good one."

Definitely a jerk. He seemed innocuous enough but, I thought, you couldn't tell from appearances alone. I was about to ask what he wanted with Celestial when he started his engine and shifted into gear. "Thanks," he said. "See you again."

He drove out of the station as Turbo waddled back from the Snack Shack, stuffing the last of a chili dog into his mouth. "That turkey ever get in touch with your mother?"

"I don't know."

The Cadillac turned up the hill toward our house. As I untangled the twisted hose, I made a mental note to ask Celestial about it when I got home.

That's when I noticed Turbo. He was bent over almost double, his shoulders shaking violently. For a second I thought he was laughing. Then I saw his lips stretched back over his teeth. His face turned purple. Was he choking on his hotdog? My God, what was that rescue technique, that squeezing maneuver we learned in health class? How could I possibly get my arms around his humongous body to squeeze him anyhow?

Turbo crumpled like a plastic bumper in a crash test while I remained frozen to the pump. I couldn't move. I couldn't think. I dropped the hose and watched a trickle of gasoline spill from the nozzle and soak into the cement by Turbo's feet.

Suddenly Skeg appeared out of nowhere. He fell to the ground, straddled Turbo's enormous stomach, and jammed his fists into Turbo's chest. "Tee! Call the fire station."

The fire station. Where the ambulance was parked. Of course. I flew into the office and shoved some junk off the desk, trying to find the stupid phone. My voice shook almost as much as my fingers, but I managed to stammer out the words. As I hung up the receiver, Gus and Larry ran across the street from the Sand Bar, the fire department annex. Skeg backed off and let them take over. Gus blew into Turbo's mouth while Larry pumped his chest. From far, far away I watched Turbo drool. Gus dragged a shirt-sleeve across Turbo's face, then breathed into his mouth again. I stumbled to the back of the station and threw up under a giant eucalyptus tree.

Leaning against the solid trunk, I heard a siren, then shouting voices and slamming doors, then the siren again as the ambulance pulled away from the station, screamed out of town, and raced up the mountain. Then I felt Skeg behind me, pulling me away from the tree, turning me around.

"Don't." I pushed my palms against his chest. "I smell awful."

"I don't care. How ya doin', babe?" he asked softly.

"Just terrific. I am so stupid. I know what to do in an emergency, but I forgot everything."

"Don't sweat it," he said, stroking my hair over and over again.

"I thought he was choking, and I couldn't figure out how to squeeze him."

"Me, too." I was glad his arms were so tight around me. My legs shook. "But when he kept grabbing his left shoulder, I guessed it was a heart attack."

I shuddered. "When did you learn CPR?"

"The summer I lifeguarded in Santa Monica."

His shoulder smelled of paint thinner and sweat. I buried my face in his neck. "I didn't know you lived in Santa Monica."

22

"Venice. The break's better in Santa Monica, but I couldn't afford to live there on a lifeguard's wages."

I sagged against his chest, feeling guilty. I couldn't believe we were having a conversation about waves and economics while Turbo was charging over the mountain road in an ambulance. "What if he dies because I panicked?"

"He's too mean to die. Come on. I'll help you close up."

He pushed Turbo's Harley into the shop while I locked the pumps, then the office and garage doors. We walked to the Lip so I could brush my teeth and get the foul taste out of my mouth. Then we went to the Sand Bar to wait for news.

Turbo made me so angry. If only he'd lost a few pounds or smoked a few less cigarettes, this wouldn't have happened. He was set for life — a good business with a steady income, a nice place to live, brains, friends. Why did he have to wreck his life? Having a weird mother was no reason to self-destruct. Believe me, I knew.

I was finishing my sixth Coke with lime wedge when Gus and Larry strolled in. Skeg bought them each a beer. They told us about Turbo regaining consciousness halfway over the mountain. "By the time we wheeled him into the emergency room, he was cracking dirty jokes and goosing the nurses," Larry said with a chuckle.

Skeg drove me home. "Do you think I should call

Turbo's mother? I mean, don't you think she'd want to know her son is in the hospital?" I asked as he swung the Whale into our driveway.

"He'd probably have another heart attack if she showed up. Or fire you for butting in."

"Well, I'm going to the hospital tomorrow. Do you want to come along?"

Despite the fact that Turbo was always harping on him for one thing or another, Skeg agreed to visit the hospital with me. I kissed him quickly on the cheek before I opened the door to the living room and pulled him inside.

Somebody sat in the tall wingback facing my mother. I could see only the back of a head, but I immediately turned around and pushed Skeg toward the doorway. "Sorry. I didn't know you had company."

"It's all right, Tee," Celestial said. "This isn't business. Come on back, you two."

She had a strange expression on her face, a cross between apprehension and excitement? Her cheeks were flushed. Maybe she had news about Turbo. Could someone have called from the bar after we left? The person in the wingback stood up and turned around — the pervert in the pink shirt! Celestial spoke tentatively. "Walter, I'd like you to meet Terra and her friend Skeg."

"Hi. We've met before, Terra, but I didn't realize you were, uh, Celestial's daughter." He grinned stupidly at me, then held out his hand to Skeg. "Craig, nice to meet you."

"It's Skeg," I corrected him, "like on a surfboard."

"What? Oh, yes." The look he gave Celestial was pathetic. If he was so embarrassed by being caught here, why had he come in the first place?

Celestial didn't move from her pile of pillows on the sofa. She wore an oversized beaded sweater and a pair of tight black pants, little embroidered Chinese shoes, large hoop earrings. As usual she looked like an exotic Gypsy. She patted the cushion beside her. "Come sit beside me, Tee. You, too, Skeg."

Like obedient puppies we traipsed across the room. Skeg sprawled on the floor and began turning a pillow over and over in his hands. When I sat down, Celestial put her hand on my shoulder. *There's something peculiar going on here,* I thought, getting more nervous by the second.

"I'm not sure how to say this, darling. You know I've always believed in being completely open and honest with you." *Say what? Is Turbo dead?* "Tee," she said softly, giving my shoulder a little squeeze. "Tee," she said again, sighing. "This is Walter Spray. Your father."

Skeg stopped turning the pillow and snapped his head into my knee. Celestial's hand fluttered around my shoulder. I looked from her to Mr. Pink and back again. I looked down at my freckled hands, then over at his sunburnt forehead. "He doesn't have freckles," I said. Then I burst into hysterical laughter.

All my life I had imagined this moment. In one version, I would be called to the principal's office and a man in a dark suit would be sitting in one of the two chairs facing the desk. He would rise when I entered the room, shake my hand formally, hold the chair for me as I sat. The principal would introduce us. He would show me a contract specifying details of parental rights and responsibilities. I would refuse to sign.

Later, when I was in my religious phase and attending services at the local Presbyterian church every Sunday, I would see him walking toward me on the beach, appearing out of the mist, bearded, and dressed in flowing white robes. He would hold out his arms and I would run to him. He would lead me into the water, saying, "I baptize you in the name of the Father and of the Daughter and of the Holy Family." Another version came to me after watching *Gone with the Wind* for the fourth time. I was Scarlett O'Hara, whirling prettily through an ornate Southern ballroom. A white-haired gentleman would tap my handsome partner on the shoulder. "May I cut in?" Of course, I would recognize him at once and, without hesitation, slap his face with a gloved hand and storm from the room.

But now, as I held onto my stomach, I just felt sick. And empty. I couldn't possibly be related to this quiet, nondescript man — this jerk! — sitting across the room. If he were truly my father, wouldn't I feel some kind of physical connection to him, a genetic bond?

His mouth twitched into a feeble smile. "I'm sorry to shock you, Tee. Celestial assured me the direct approach would be best. I'm sorry. I hope we can get to know each other. Not all at once. I realize I can't expect you to make room for me in your life immediately. But I hope we can spend a little time together." He rolled his hands over on the arms of the wingback so the palms faced the ceiling, almost as if he were begging.

Suddenly a great wave of tiredness swept over me. Between Turbo's heart attack and this absurd revelation, I felt like a massive piece of waterlogged driftwood.

"Excuse me. I'm going to bed now." I sounded like a four year old. I shook off my mother's hand and leaned briefly on the top of Skeg's head for balance as I stood up. Then I crossed the floor, through the path of the jerk's entreating gaze, walked into my room and closed the door. Mao, our ancient Siamese, flicked his tail from beneath my pillow. I popped a cassette into my Walkman and lay down, pulling the cat onto my chest. Mao purred while I listened to Sting sing about the wives and daughters of the disappeareds in Chile dancing with photographs of their missing loved ones. "Dancing with their fathers . . . They dance alone."

27

Chapter 3

My mother was a hippie. In 1969 she graduated from Cal and moved into a house in the Berkeley hills with three friends.

The four young women weren't cultural dropouts or welfare leeches. They had all earned degrees in fine arts and supported themselves with their artwork. On the political side, they marched and sat down and spoke out and sang protest songs and wrote letters to their congressmen. I suppose they burned bras, too.

Eventually they grew tired of the burned-out acid freaks in People's Park and the chanting Hare Krishnas of Sproul Plaza. They became almost as troubled by the growing violence of the Vietnam protesters as they were by the war itself.

One Sunday they happened to drive through Arena Beach. Arena's cottages reminded Betsy of her Cape Cod girlhood. Friendly residents made Karen homesick for New Orleans. The outlying ranches resembled the farm in Iowa where Carla had grown up. My mother took one look at Arena and knew she'd found a home.

Within a month, they rented an old farmhouse, built before the 1906 earthquake by one of the town's original Portuguese founders, and settled in. Betsy hauled her looms into the barn and purchased a pair of sheep from the landlord. Karen set up her wheel in an old shed and built a brick kiln for firing her gourd-like ceramic musical instruments. Carla converted the wide back porch into a painting studio. My mother arranged her beading and embroidery materials in the long upstairs room under the eaves.

They called their new commune Harmony House.

On the anniversary of their first year in residence, the four friends celebrated. They agreed, over bowls of lentil soup and a loaf of sprouted-wheat bread, to take on new names reflecting their new lives. Betsy blossomed into Rose Petal. Karen metamorphosed into Monarch Grove. Carla discovered she was Serenity personified. And my mother, born Nancy Josephina Jankowski, and the only child of Master Sergeant Joseph Jakob Jankowski and Maya Ruth Hansen, transmuted into Celestial Bliss.

"Tell again how you met my father," I said for the hundredth time since I'd grown old enough to be curious about him. I sat on a rug woven by Rose and watched my mother string together bits of punctured lapis, shimmering glass beads, and thin silver cylinders. She held an unfinished earring up to my cheek, leaned back in an old willow rocker, and twisted the thread in her hand so the beads caught the light and threw sparkles on the walls and ceiling. She pursed her lips and chose another few beads from the antique sewing chest she'd inherited from her mother.

"Many years ago, two gigantic, evil sea monsters battled in a winter fog as thick and cold as vichyssoise. Thick black blood poured from their bellies into the ocean and spread up and down the coast. The sands of Arena Beach turned black."

I snuggled closer to her. "Tell it the real way, Celestial, not like a fairy tale."

She smiled and shook her head at me. "All right. The night Serenity, Monarch, Rose, and I chose our new names, two Standard Oil tankers collided under the Golden Gate Bridge. The next evening I was in the Sand Bar with tears running down my cheeks and dripping into my wine glass when this very straight-looking man walked in the door and sat down beside me. He wore brand-new hiking boots and khaki pants, a flannel shirt, and down vest."

"Was he handsome, Celestial?"

"Not like Redford or Newman, certainly, but kind-looking, gentle."

"Then you saw his badge?"

"Then he ordered a drink, a Wild Turkey straight up."

"And then?"

"That's when I saw the badge on his vest with the Standard Oil logo."

"And that's when you spilled your wine?"

"That's when I spilled my wine. I'd spent all day rescuing birds from the oil, listening to their pitiful mewling, cleaning out their nostrils with Q-tips. I never even realized birds had nostrils before I watched a grebe struggle for air in my arms. Oh, Tee, it was awful. Hundreds of them. We cleaned them and put them in cardboard boxes. Then somebody came and took them away to a recovery center." Celestial cupped the earring in her hands, hands to her breast, and let the needle fall to her lap. Her eyes always got wet when she came to this part of the story. Her eyes were so beautiful when she was sad, big pools of blue, like cerulean puddles on Serenity's palette.

"And most of them died anyway?" I asked, wanting to prolong the moment of pure remorse in those eyes.

She nodded. "Poor things, covered with that thick, black oil. It was like molasses, only worse, because water wouldn't wash it away. We had to soak them in mineral oil to loosen it, then drag cornmeal through their feathers and rub out as much of the mess as we could."

31

I put my chin on her knee and she patted my head absentmindedly. "Watch out for the needle," she whispered.

For a minute or so we were quiet. Then I began to rub my chin into the soft flesh beneath her skirt. "So you spilled the wine on my father's pants."

"Yes," she said, a tiny smile tugging at the corners of her lips. Now her eyes sparkled like the unfinished earrings. "I refused to sit beside this horrible industrial polluter for one more second, so I spun around on the bar stool and accidentally knocked my glass right onto his lap."

I could see him jumping up indignantly, brushing his thighs, demanding a towel from the bartender. I held my breath, waiting for Celestial to continue.

"'The wine I can handle. It's the salt from the tears that stings,' he said as he mopped up the floor. His hair had thick swatches of black oil in it. When he stood up I could see how tired he was. But I couldn't stand that hangdog expression on his face, so I left the bar without saying another word."

As the oil cleanup progressed over the next few weeks, Celestial and Walter found themselves working side-by-side to save Arena. Heated conversations about big business and the government war machine evolved somehow into a brief and steamy romance.

I was born nine months later in the kitchen of Harmony House. A midwife supervised the event and made certain all was safe and sanitary. Rose coached Celestial's breathing, Monarch brewed gallons of herb tea, and Serenity sketched the various stages of labor. My mother always said my birth was Harmony's best and most productive labor of love.

"Tell me my father's name," I demanded as my mother hoed the weeds in our vegetable garden.

"His name is Walter. You know that."

Yes, I knew. I had asked the question many times.

"Why isn't he here, Celestial?"

"Because he had to go away."

"Why?"

She leaned on her hoe and sighed. "I can't answer that question. It's very complicated, and I'm not sure I understand it myself." She pulled a carrot from the ground and handed it to me. I wiped it on my shorts and bit off the end, tasting sweet orange flesh and dirt.

"Where did he go?"

"He went to war."

War. I knew about war from my friend Sasha's television set and from a song that Celestial and Rose sang about young men and girls, flowers and soldiers and graveyards.

"Is my father dead?"

"I don't know."

"But why don't you know, Celestial?"

"Because no one ever told me, sweetheart."

I munched on the juicy carrot. Of course he was

dead. If he were alive, he would come to see me. I knew that in my four-year-old heart, where all knowledge is certain.

Celestial was always spacy, unfocused, or else focused on something far beyond the rest of us even then. She created fantastic jewelry and clothing, adorned with beads and sequins, festooned with intricate embroidery, but was never good at completing an order on schedule. Most of her private customers thought her attitude very artistic, but the big stores — Saks, Magnin's, City of Paris — canceled her contracts.

We were two sides of the same coin, my mother and I. Celestial and Terra Bliss — heavenly and earthly happiness. While Celestial built castles in the sky, I constructed sturdy ranch houses on the sands of Arena Beach.

There was never a shortage of men at Harmony House. Although Rose and Monarch shared a room and a bed, they had lots of male as well as female visitors, friends from college traveling the coast. Serenity always seemed to have a man in residence. For a few years, her friend Sebastian lived with us. Sebastian played the sitar, strange music that gave me headaches. After Sebastian came Othello, a part-time drama teacher at San Francisco State. Then David the stockbroker moved in. Serenity called them her old men, even though some of them were younger than she was. Mostly they were nice to be around. They played chess or poker with me, when they weren't too stoned or too busy making music or love or deals. None of them ever mistreated me.

My mother had occasional male friends, too, but they never spent more than a night or two. When I asked her why she didn't want them to stay longer, to move in with us, she said she didn't love them enough. "I'd have to love someone a great deal to be able to live with him. I love Serenity and Monarch and Rose. And I love you more than anyone, Ti-ti. That's more love than most people find in a lifetime."

I was very fortunate. I had a mother who loved me deeply, if distractedly, and three live-in adult friends who were almost like older sisters or aunts. What more did I need? Certainly not a father.

Rose taught me to ride a bicycle and, when I grew big enough, to chop kindling. Monarch showed me how to fix things. Together we repaired a toaster that burned our bread to a crisp, a tape deck that refused to fast forward, a window broken when Celestial was teaching me how to pitch a baseball.

I learned as much as anyone with two parents and didn't spend a whole lot of time thinking about my missing father. Except on rare occasions. Like the time at the playground I saw a man grab a little boy by the waist and swing him into the air, the boy's hair lifting and flying into his face, his mouth wide open, squealing. I wondered how it felt to be picked up and swung like that by a pair of hairy, masculine arms. Even though I was deathly afraid of heights, I would have liked to try it. Just once. And there was the time I saw a man on the beach fishing with a girl about my age. He crouched behind her and wrapped his hand over her wrist. I could almost feel his beard rub my cheek. He drew her arm back with his own, pulled the pole through the air and flipped the baited hook into the water just beyond the surf line. I watched it splash, then turned away and kicked a rock all the way down the beach.

About the time my breasts began developing, the mellow music of Harmony House began to change, too. Rose, the leader of our chorus, grew especially discordant. She criticized Monarch's cooking, complained about Celestial's daydreaming, and mocked Serenity's dependence on men.

One day as Serenity and David sunbathed in the nude on the barn roof, they got into a huge argument. David yelled and Serenity cried. When Serenity climbed down from the barn, she ran inside with a large red welt on her cheek. Rose gave David an hour to get out of town.

For a while the house was peaceful again. Then a group of jazz musicians — old pals of Serenity's friend Sebastian — crashed in the parlor. They jammed all night and slept most of the day. They ate all the food in the refrigerator, grazed the garden like a herd of goats, wiped out the supply of homemade preserves on the shelves, and left their dirty dishes all over the kitchen. Rose, this time with Monarch's backing, confronted Serenity and told her the band would have to go. Serenity offered to pay the food bill, but Rose stood firm. She couldn't work in such chaos. The musicians packed up their instruments that night. Serenity drove off into the sunset with them, her easel, canvases, and paints crammed in the back of their van.

My mother remained unfazed by the disturbances. Complacent as always, regarding whatever came her way as her Karma, she retreated to her upstairs room and worked on a bead-and-feather wall hanging for a Taos art dealer.

A few weeks later, just as everything but my body was getting back to normal, Rose took Monarch's hand across the dinner table and announced that they were moving to Oregon. "We've decided to join the Bhagwan Rajneesh."

Celestial and I combed Arena for a new home. When I spotted a FOR RENT sign on a tiny house on the hill, Celestial promised to sew diligently so we could afford it. I kept my fingers crossed and worked out a family budget.

"Celestial, how can I find the square root of a hundred thirty-nine?" I asked. Rain pelted the roof and occasional gusts of wind rattled the door, but we were snug inside our cozy cottage. The light from the fireplace flickered over my math book and turned the gown Celestial was beading for a Hollywood film star into a sky of glittering constellations. Mao stalked a sow bug across the hearth.

Since our move the year before, my mother had grown increasingly distant and withdrawn. At first her mental retreats simply irritated me. Then I began to worry. Was she sick? What could I do to help her get well?

That night, when she didn't answer my square-root question, I closed my math book in frustration and looked up. Celestial's hand, still holding a needle with a few black beads on it, was suspended in the air. Her eyes were half closed, unseeing. She began to speak in a voice that was not hers, a voice that scared the pants off me.

"Roots are never square. Intricate webs of support, they nourish and defend," the strange voice said. Mao's tail looked like a bottle brush as he arched his back and hissed. Then he dashed across my math book and vanished into my room. "You find your roots where you plant your soul."

"Celestial?"

No answer.

"Celestial!" I jumped up and shook her shoulders. "Wake up!"

She blinked her eyes, then opened them wide and

smiled at me. "Did you say something, darling?"

"You were talking in your sleep."

"I was?" she asked, looking surprised and amused at the same time. "What did I say?"

"I don't remember."

"You don't remember any of it?"

"Well," I reluctantly admitted, "you said something about roots."

"Oh. Well, roots are important. Any army brat can tell you that. Did I say anything else?"

I shook my head.

"What did I sound like?"

"Like an old man far away. A ghost."

When I began to cry, she set the gown on the table beside her and pulled me onto her lap, even though I was almost as big as she was by then. "Don't be frightened. It's all right," she murmured, stroking my hair. "Sometimes a very wise spirit visits me. He won't hurt you. His name is Astraeus. He wants to tell you something."

"This wasn't a spirit. It was you. You were the one talking."

"Are you sure, Tee?"

"Tell him to go away," I sniffed, staring at the fire, not sure of anything.

She rocked me back and forth. "I'm afraid I can't do that, Tee. Astraeus has many things to say and he has chosen me to be his channel." She kissed my cheek and put me down. "If you want to pretend it's me talking, if that will make you less scared, I don't think he'll mind."

"How can I pretend it's you when you talk in that creepy voice?"

And how could I not be scared when I was in one world and the person I loved most was in another?

Channel. I looked up the word in the big dictionary in the school library. There was nothing about getting in touch with another dimension or receiving information from a spirit. The dictionary talked about conveying through or directing toward a particular course, excavating a groove. A backhoe channels a ditch in the earth.

Channeler was not even listed.

The more demented my mother grew, the more I thought about my missing father. If he were alive, how could I find him? Celestial couldn't even remember the name of the town where he'd grown up. I considered phoning the Red Cross, the Veteran's Administration, the child abuse hot line. But I didn't want any government social worker snooping around.

Besides, I wasn't absolutely positive that I wanted to locate my father. What if he didn't like me? What if I didn't like him? What if he liked me and decided to get into a custody battle with my mother?

What if I discovered he was dead?

Somehow not knowing became safer than knowing, and instead of taking any real action, I reconciled myself to dealing with Celestial's behavior alone. But as she got crazier and crazier, I began writing letters in my diary.

Dear Mr. Spray,

You don't know me, but my name is Terra. Remember the oil spill? Remember Celestial? Well, your spilled oil and her spilled wine caused more than dead birds and dirty pants. Maybe we could get together some time and talk things over.

Your daughter,
Terra Bliss

Dear Walter,

Thank you for the note. It was nice to hear from you and to get the picture of you and your wife.

I would be happy to visit you next summer.

Sincerely,
Terra

Dear Dad,

How are you? I am fine. I am twelve years old now. I look just like you except my conscience is clear.

Love,
Tee

Dearest Papa,

*How kind of you to send me the airplane
ticket. Please accept my humble thanks. I am
afraid I will be unable to visit you next month. I
put the ticket to very good use, but it clogged up
our plumbing.*

Your loving daughter,
Terrable Bliss

Hi Pops!

*I'm having a great time at good old Camp
Sappho. We sew and cook and scrub the cabins
every day. All the counselors and campers are female. We don't allow men to pollute the atmos-
phere.*

Hugs and kisses,
Terra Firma

Dear Mr. Spray,

*You don't know me, but you used to know my
mother well. I think she is insane.*

On my thirteenth birthday, Celestial suggested a hike
up Deep Ravine, one of the canyons that cut into the
mountain above Arena. We followed the trail beside a
small creek. After a mile or so, we sat down on a
smooth rocky shelf, removed our shoes and socks,
and dipped our feet into the still water. In the hush

of the redwood forest, a Stellar's jay screeched.

Celestial drew an envelope from her pocket. "I've been saving this for you. Happy Birthday, darling." The envelope, postmarked Detroit, Michigan, March 9, 1971, was addressed to Celestial. Willing my hands to stop trembling, I pulled out the letter inside, unfolded it, and began to read.

Dear Celestial,

Here I am in my old bedroom (ducks and hunters on the wallpaper), surrounded by my rock collection and baseball cards and fishing gear, thinking about Arena Beach and you.

Shortly after our last "discussion," I came back to Michigan and spent a few weeks with my folks, contemplating my future. The day before I was due to be inducted into the army, I signed up for OCS. I figured I'd rather be a lieutenant than a private. I guess I was also hoping the war might be over before I completed the extra training. Now, after Basic, OCS, and AIT (that's Advanced Infantry Training, in case you've forgotten your army lingo), my time is up.

I received orders for Vietnam last week.

It's still not too late to go to Canada, as you encouraged me to do a century ago. The bridge across the Detroit River to Ontario isn't far away and, even if my name were to appear on a "no

*exit" list there, I could drive to the Upper Penin-
sula (remember me telling you how my dad and I
used to fish the U.P. when I was a kid?) and cross
the border easily.*

   *But I'm not going to run away. We all know
that this war has been unfairly fought by the
lower classes. Even with the lottery, I still hear
about my old fraternity brothers and the sons of
my parents' friends getting deferred for a variety
of reasons (most having to do with where they
played golf or went to law school).*

   *I've had a lot of time (scrubbing barracks
floors, spit-polishing boots, shooting cardboard
targets) to think about what you finally said
about the war. But I'm no closer to agreeing with
you now than I was a year ago. I still believe we
were right to come to South Vietnam's aid in the
first place. I also think we should have blasted
the devil out of the North and gotten out of the
country long ago. But we didn't.*

   *Now the powers that be in Washington have
pulled my name out of a hat and said it is my
turn to participate. Why should someone else go
in my place? I am no hero, but maybe I'm a bit
older and a tad wiser than some of those young
recruits fresh out of high school. Who knows?
Maybe I can even save one or two lives.*

   I'm scared (especially after finding out the

44

*mortality rate for lieutenants) and hopeful at the
same time. Maybe this war will end sooner than
it would if only gung-ho supporters were in, skep-
tics and dissidents out.*

*Back in California (was it only a year ago
that I first looked into your blue eyes?), I told you
I didn't want to be burdened by any unnecessary
emotional ties if I had to go to Nam. I'm sorry if
that sounded cold. Know that you were, and still
are, a precious part of my life.*

With fond memories,
Walter

So this was my father — this envelope, these three
pieces of paper. These words. His handwriting was
regular and neat, on a slight backward slant. He collected rocks and baseball cards and liked to fish. He
was no hero. If he'd known about me, would he have
considered me an unnecessary emotional burden, too?
I reread it and started to ask Celestial why she had
waited so long to show it to me, but she was staring off
into space, traveling again.

Over the next months, I opened and closed that letter so many times the pages became dirty, the creases
worn. Finally, on the day of my graduation from junior
high, I taped the rips together and placed the letter in
an empty tea cannister with a single crystal earring, a
World War II photograph of my grandfather in his

army uniform, and my diary. I buried the can under a Eureka lemon tree in our back yard.

At fourteen, I blamed my mother for everything — my bony knees, my mousy hair, my difficulty making friends, and, most of all, my father's disappearance. If she hadn't been such a hippie, he never would have left her. If she had told him she was pregnant, he certainly would have married her. If she hadn't argued with him about the war, he would have come back to us both after Vietnam.

"I can't believe you never tried to find him."

"Tee, he knew where I lived. If he wanted to reach me, he could have. There was no point trying to force him to come back. If he returned out of guilt or a sense of obligation . . ."

"Obligation like me, you mean?"

"Like you. Or me." She stared off into space for a minute. "We were very different, your father and I. Not our backgrounds — we both came from conservative, middle-class families who believed in God and country. But we saw things so differently. I'm not saying that one of us was right and the other wrong. But our staying together was like trying to mix oil and water. Does that make sense?"

Oil and water. Oil and vinegar. I'd made enough mayonnaise to know that, if you mixed them right, even oil and vinegar would blend together. It was called emulsification.

46

"You don't even know if he got killed over there."
My voice was belligerent, accusatory. "How can you
stand not knowing whether the father of your child is
alive or dead?"

"What difference would it make, darling?"

"Well, it makes one heck of a big difference to me.
Just because you hated your father didn't give you any
right to deprive me of mine."

She looked at me wide-eyed, then went back to
needlepointing some stupid mandala. I could have
punched her for her complacency, her go-with-the-
flow acceptance of whatever happened to her. Her
Karma. Argh! I stormed from the house and slammed
the door in her Karmic face.

A few days later I began calling Michigan information, starting with Ann Arbor. There was no Walter
Spray listed there, or in Battle Creek, Bay City, Detroit, East Lansing, Flint, Grand Rapids, Kalamazoo,
Pontiac, or Port Huron. After the tenth phone call, I
gave up. Maybe Celestial was right. What difference
would it make if I found him? I didn't want a father
who felt obligated to me. Besides, Celestial and I
didn't need anyone else. Did we?

All my life my mother let me make my own decisions.
She never told me what to do, just let me learn from
my own mistakes (like the awful time I got loaded on
cooking sherry when I was fifteen). Celestial never
tried to foist her own opinions on me either, about pol-

itics or sex or drugs or anything else. I suppose she was trying to be a different kind of parent than her father, the drill sergeant, had been. Mostly I appreciated her attitude and realized how lucky I was, compared to my friend Sasha, for instance, whose mother was always telling her what to wear and how to comb her hair and who she could and couldn't go out with. But sometimes I hated my independence. Just once I wanted Celestial to say, if you do this, then that will follow. Or even better, to be told to do something. Or ordered not to.

The night my father reappeared in Arena Beach, I tucked Mao under my chin and lay awake for hours, aching for some direction in my life.

Chapter 4

I woke up in darkness and heard them talking. Celestial and him. Walter. Mr. Pink. My father. I whispered the word in Mao's ear. He opened half an eye suspiciously, then twitched his ears, shook his head, and went back to sleep, curled into the curve of my body.

The next time I surfaced, the house was quiet. Had he gone? Maybe I'd imagined the whole thing in the aftershock of Turbo's heart attack. And what about Turbo? Was he still alive, still kicking and swearing and telling dirty jokes?

Finally, after an agony of hours, the world outside my window took shape. I tucked Mao back under the covers and crept to the phone.

"I'm calling about Mr. Turbo O'Neil," I said, making my voice high and shaky, old-womanish. What if they gave out information only to relatives? "He was admitted yesterday."

"We have a Francis Aloysius O'Neil listed. Is that the patient about whom you are inquiring?"

Francis Aloysius! Score another point for Turbo's mother. "Yes, that's the one. Dear little Francis, my grandson."

"Mr. O'Neil is still in ICU, madam. His condition is listed as fair."

"When may I see him?"

"As soon as he is released from ICU, madam, during our regular visiting hours — twelve to four and six to eight."

"Thanks," I said in my own voice, hanging up quickly. I grabbed an apple from the basket on the kitchen counter and let myself out the front door. No brown Cadillac lay in wait on the street. I started the Whale and motored down the hill to the station.

In the depths of the desk clutter, I found Turbo's clipboard with the day's schedule. Jones — lube and oil. No problem. Texeira — rings. I'd have to ask Tex to reschedule. I'd only done one ring job, and that with Turbo standing beside me the whole time. Better not risk it alone. Pursey — algnmt & tires. Easy. Shaffer or Shatter, or some other name I couldn't decipher and didn't recognize, had a trannie knock he or she wanted looked at. Better postpone that one, too. The bell dinged in the shop. I went outside to pump enough gas for Bill Mundy to get over the mountain to his job at the central post office in the city. Then, between customers, I hosed down the cement, located the keys to

50

Bob Pursey's car under the driver's seat, drove it into the garage and jacked it up.

I was busy all morning and measured time passing by the increasing rumbles emanating from my stomach. Except for the apple I'd devoured on my way to work, I hadn't eaten anything since lunch yesterday, and the remnants of that I'd deposited under the eucalyptus behind the shop.

Skeg came by around ten-thirty to ask if I had any news on Turbo. I told him about my phone call and sent him to the Snack Shack for a cheese and chili omelette and strawberry shake.

"I saw your, uh, father's car parked in the beach lot when I came out of the water earlier," he said, handing me a foil-covered paper plate.

"Well, he'd better not come around here," I said around a huge bite of omelette. I chewed and swallowed. "God, he's such a jerk." Skeg didn't say anything. "Don't you think he's a jerk?"

Skeg shrugged, then kissed me on the lips — how embarrassing, right next to the unleaded pump! — and headed for the surf shop.

I could see him standing outside the wide-open shop door. "How was the beach?" I asked, jabbing the lube gun at the grease fittings of Will Jones's Accord.

He grinned stupidly. "No secrets in a small town, right?"

"That's right, Walt."

He sipped a cup of coffee — take-out from the Snack Shack. "I'd forgotten how pretty the beach can be early in the morning. There were some big birds diving into the water. Really big birds."

"Pelicans."

"I don't remember them from when I was here back in 'seventy-one. Managing the oil spill cleanup."

"Wasn't the oil spill in January? The pelicans wouldn't have been here then." And you didn't stick around long enough to see them. "They're seasonal." I wiped a glob of grease off Will's left front tire. "Did you know that pelicans mate for life?" Out of the corner of my eye I saw him wince.

"No, I don't know much about birds."

Or about much else, I thought. "So, Wally, how long are you planning to stay in Arena Beach?"

"I'm not sure, Tee. That depends partly on you."

"Well, it's a free country."

"In some respects." He took off his glasses and began to rub them with a handkerchief he pulled from the pocket of his slacks. "Can't seem to keep these darn things clean."

I hoped I hadn't inherited his eyesight. "Why don't you get contacts if your glasses are such a pain?"

"According to my ophthalmologist, I'm one of the ten percent who can't wear them." He leaned against the door jamb and gazed up at the mountain. "That was one of the first things I noticed about your mother — her blue eyes."

Was that before or after you screwed her, I wanted to ask. Instead, I opened the hood of Will's Honda and hid inside.

"Your mother invited me to stay with you."

"With me?"

"With both of you. In your house."

"We don't have a guest room."

"I know, but she insisted. To tell you the truth, I appreciate the offer. I'm afraid my bed at the Dunes will be carried off by ants while I sleep."

I pulled Will's dipstick. "Did Celestial tell you she works at home?"

"Yes, she mentioned that. I'll clear out during the day so I won't be in her way."

"Did she mention what she does for a living?"

"Yes. And she told me you don't approve."

I eased the dipstick back in its shaft. "Well, what do you think, Walt? Do you approve? Or do you think she's crazy?"

"It's a free country."

I glanced at him sharply, but he was still staring at the mountain. I couldn't tell if he was being sincere or sarcastic.

"Well, then," he said, starting to walk away, "I'll let you get back to work." He turned around. "By the way, your Skig seems like a nice fellow."

"It's Skeg, S–K–E–G, and he's not mine, and you have no right to approve or disapprove of anyone I see."

53

"I'm sorry, Tee. I didn't mean it that way." He fiddled with a button on his shirt. "See you later?"

I didn't answer.

Turbo reminded me of one of those beached whales. Sometimes well-meaning people maneuver the huge beasts back into the water where they belong, but the whales just drift toward shore and beach themselves again. Eventually they die.

Turbo had this glazed, bewildered look on his face, as if he didn't understand why he was in the hospital. He overwhelmed the narrow bed. Tubes and wires sprouted from his arms and drooped from his nostrils. A television mounted high on the wall broadcast a loud game of "Jeopardy!", but Turbo didn't pay any attention to it until he noticed Skeg and me watching him from the door. Then he rolled his eyes from us to the TV and back again.

"The young swashbuckler who never grew up," he said hoarsely.

"Peter Pan." I plopped into a plastic chair beside his bed.

"You didn't give your response in the form of a question. That's five hundred dollars off your score, sucker." He pushed the mute button on the remote, then winced and closed his eyes.

"Want your pillows fluffed?"

"Keep your filthy hands off. I'm paying these uni-

54

formed idiots a bloody fortune to fluff my pillows, and I don't want you doing their job."

I was glad to see him in such good spirits, but he looked terrible. His face was pale and oily, his arms bruised.

I started telling him about the work I'd done at the station that day. I didn't mention the difficulties I had aligning Bob Pursey's front end or the hour I spent trying to find a critical nut lost somewhere in the depths of Mrs. Henry's Volvo engine compartment.

Turbo nodded off as I talked and soon began to snore.

I joined Skeg at the wide windowsill where he sat watching the parking lot five stories below. Looking down that far made me dizzy, so I wedged my hips between Skeg's knees and listened to Turbo snore.

A nurse came in, looked at Turbo's chart, smiled at us, and went out again. An old man in a plaid robe and slippers pushed a walker down the hall. His head jerked from side to side with each step. Then a young couple went past the door, arguing about something. The woman clenched her hands tightly and the man kept pulling on his face. I wondered if my mother and father would have fought like that if they'd stayed together. Probably not. Celestial wasn't the arguing type. But what kind of marriage would they have had?

I could picture us in some suburban tract house. Walter would go off to work every morning, briefcase in hand. Celestial, whose name would be Nancy again, would kiss him good-bye at the door in her tennis outfit — a little short skirt, pastel blouse, visor over her styled hair. I'd walk to school and gossip with my friends. I'd spend summers on a lake and go to homecoming dances and parties and basketball games and get straight A's.

I snorted.

"What?" Skeg said.

"I was thinking about where I'd be now if Celestial had married Walter."

"Where?"

"Not working on cars in Arena Beach, that's for sure."

Skeg grinned. "Did you see him today?"

"He came snooping around the station. Celestial invited him to stay with us." I bit off a ragged hangnail and examined my hands. My fingernails were lined with dirty grease, my knuckles scraped. I could just imagine what Walter thought about his daughter, the mechanic.

"Well, you can always move in with me, babe. No strings attached." He took a bashed-up hand and kissed the knuckles.

"No fornicating allowed in front of heart patients," Turbo grunted from the bed. "Upsets the old ticker." He patted his chest. "And who the hell is Walter?"

I told him briefly about yesterday's second shock. "I

wouldn't trust any jackass who drives a Cadillac," he pronounced with an open mind.

Just then the nurse returned and told us we'd have to leave. Visiting hours were over.

"Besides that, I've got to attend to some extremely private affairs," he said, waving a thick arm toward a bedpan in the corner. "And you've got to get to bed early so you can wake up and go to school tomorrow."

"But I'm not —"

"Don't give me any lip. I'm a sick man." He winked. "As you have so often told me."

"Anything you say, boss." I tweaked his toe under the bedcovers and headed for the door, resolving to cut school again and keep the station running despite what he said.

"Skeg?" I heard Turbo croak.

"Yo, dude?"

"Thanks for yesterday."

Skeg was still smiling when he came out of the room, grabbed my hand, and headed for the elevators.

On the way back to Arena, I considered staying at the Lip with Skeg, but I didn't want to leave Celestial alone with Walter. I dropped Skeg in town and drove up the hill.

When I walked into the house, Walter was spreading an old sleeping bag on the living room couch. "Hello there."

"Where's Celestial?"

"She went for a walk to clear her head before bed."

They'd probably set this up so I'd have to talk to him. I went into the kitchen and poured an orange juice on the rocks.

"That sleeping bag is mildewed," I said at the same time he asked, "How is your friend Turbo?"

We both stopped. Then he spoke again. "What did you say?"

"Nothing important."

He sat down on his sleeping bag and picked up a magazine from the floor. I sipped my juice.

"What are you —"

"Why did you —"

He put the magazine down. "Let's take turns. You first."

I stuck my finger in my glass, pulled out an ice cube, popped it in my mouth, and sucked on it, staring at him. I still had a difficult time believing that this person was actually my father. So far he'd done nothing to deserve the term except sleep with my mother eighteen years ago.

If he wasn't my father in any but the merest accidental way, what was he then? Someone else's father? Husband?

"Are you married?"

"Yes, I am." He put his stockinged feet on the coffee table. "My turn?"

I nodded.

"Are you married?" he asked, one eyebrow raised.

I eyeballed him over the top of my glass. "Divorced," I told him. "Twice." He didn't look quite so dorky when he grinned.

"Your turn," he said.

"What's your wife's name?"

"Wendy."

"Wendy?" For some reason this struck me as hilarious. "Great. A Wendy Wife. Just like Peter Pan. Wendy and Walter. Do you have your initials on your license plate?"

"That's two questions in a row for you. Unfair."

"Well, this is getting pretty boring, Walter, so just forget I asked, okay?" The words slipped out before I even thought about them.

He blinked at me stupidly, then riffled through his *Sports Illustrated*. I fished another ice cube from my glass.

He folded the magazine in half and tapped it on his thigh, then sighed. "Look, Tee, I'm not a complete idiot. Nor am I entirely without feelings. If we're going to get anywhere with this conversation, if you have any interest in talking with me, you'll have to take that chip off your shoulder and start treating me like a human being instead of some insensate moron."

I crunched the ice cube between my molars. "He walks, he talks, he feels. Give this man the Father-of-the-Year award," I said mildly. His face grew redder and redder; he squeezed the magazine tightly. Was he going to hit me? I'd like to see him try. Who did he think he was, barging into our lives, making demands? I rubbed an ice cube across my lips till they were numb. "Sorry. I didn't mean that." Didn't I? I could almost hear the ice melting in my fingers, the room was so quiet.

"That's quite a car you drive," he said finally, tossing the magazine on the floor. "Had it long?"

I knew he was only making small talk, trying to soften me up and get me to like him, but I told him about the Whale anyhow. It was easier to talk about cars than about anything personal.

"I used to drive a VW bug when I was at Michigan State studying economics." It figured. He was the type to major in money.

"I thought Michigan State was just for jocks." I made a face at him so he'd know I was joking.

"That's the propaganda from Ann Arbor. No, it's quite a highly respected school. In fact, we used to have more Rhodes scholars than any other school in the country."

Wow, Walt, I'm impressed. But I didn't say it. He looked too helpless and dorky, sitting there with the spare tire under his polo shirt hanging over a pair of brand new Levi's he'd probably bought just to cultivate a casual image. He'd come all the way out here to look up an old girlfriend (did that mean that he and Wendy Wife were having problems?) and discovered a daughter he never knew about. A rude, nasty daughter at that. I knew I should make allowances for what must have been a tremendous shock to him, but somehow I didn't feel that I was the one who should be understanding.

Just then the front door opened and Celestial stepped in. "What a beautiful night. So clear I thought Orion's belt would reach down and touch my hair." She kept talking about the stars while she hung her cape in the closet, kicked off her shoes, and sat down on the couch beside Walter, covering his hand with her own. "Do you remember that morning we drove up on the mountain to see the full moon set and the sun rise at the same time?"

He smiled and gave her hand a squeeze. Was this how married people acted? For a second my throat had this huge baseball in it. Then Celestial freed her hand from his and the lump slowly dissolved.

"Did you and Skeg manage to see Turbo? How is he? I imagine he was delighted to have company. How soon will he be out?" Before I could answer, she continued. "What about the station? And school? Are you planning to cut classes tomorrow?"

There she was, my mother, not telling me what to do or even making suggestions, but simply asking a string of questions about my plans. Great. "Tomorrow and Friday. Next week is spring break. By the time school starts again, Turbo'll probably be back at work."

"I'd be happy to give you a hand," Walter said.

"I'm not exactly a mechanical genius — especially when it comes to cars — but I could pump gas and free you for the more complicated jobs."

"Thanks, but I can manage myself."

"I'm sure you can, Tee." Those pleading eyes again. I remembered how frantic I'd been all day and had to admit — at least to myself — that an extra pair of hands would be useful. What did I have to lose?

"If you want to come down and help during commute hours, I guess that would be all right."

He smiled. "What time do we open?"

He wasn't on the couch when I got up the next morning. His sleeping bag looked like an abandoned cocoon and was cold to my touch. That could mean one of two things. Either he had risen early and gone out before my alarm went off, or he had moved into Celestial's room during the night.

I listened at Celestial's door on my way to the bathroom but couldn't tell if more than one person breathed in her bed. Parents were supposed to sleep together, I thought as I brushed my teeth and examined a fresh zit in the mirror. Even so, if that man had slept with my mother, I'd wring both their necks.

He came in the front door while I was finishing my granola. "That Snack Shack makes great coffee," he said, setting a paper cup with a plastic lid on the table and sitting down opposite me.

"Caffeine kills brain cells."

"Ah, but it puts hair on your head," he said, "and my head can use all the help it can get." He smoothed a long thin strand across the top of his skull and down toward his left ear.

"You can say that again," I said in a friendly sort of way.

Between customers we talked about the weather, the traffic, the tourists. I changed the oil on Sid Chambers's Rover, patched a tire for old Mrs. Deets, and found a new set of plugs for Bill Stuart's Mustang in a cluttered drawer under the workbench. The morning commute rush dwindled to a trickle, but I didn't tell Walter to go away. He was actually kind of funny, and I was — despite myself — beginning to enjoy his company.

I should have known better.

"So, what colleges have you applied to? Your mother tells me you're quite a good student."

Yeah, great, Walt. Last semester I got an A− in physics, an A in auto shop, a B in statistics, a C+ in English, and quite a good F in French. Comprennez-vous? "I'm not going to college."

I glanced over my shoulder to see what my alleged father would do with that bit of information. He jerked his head like a spastic. The long, hopeful lock of hair flipped into his open mouth. He extracted the hair and circled it into place over his cranium. "Any particular reason?"

I yanked a plug wire off Bill's Mustang. "Hand me the plug wrench from that drawer, will you? No, the longer one." The plug stuck tightly but I finally managed to loosen it. When I showed the carbon-covered tip to Walter, he nodded as if he knew what the black deposit meant. "College would be just a waste of time and money for someone like me."

I struggled with the second plug, which was practically welded on.

Walter spoke softly. "Well, college isn't the answer for everyone."

The plug came free suddenly. "Damn!" I yelled as my knuckles smashed into the block. Walter raised an eyebrow in my direction, then crawled under the car to retrieve the wrench.

Don't talk to me about answers, I said to his back as I swallowed the stupid lump in my throat, mad at him for not caring enough to tell me what to do, knowing I'd be even angrier if he had.

Chapter 5

Walter pumped gas and washed windshields while I tried to keep up with the shop work. Between fill-ups and oil changes, I learned that he drove a Ford Taurus sedan with forty thousand miles, Wendy a new Oldsmobile station wagon. He backed the Tigers and the Pistons. Wendy hated television sports. They both liked Italian food better than Chinese, Greek best of all. Their favorite restaurant was a tiny cafe called the Acropolis that made the best dolmas and moussaka this side of Athens, according to Walter. I thought I might try my hand at moussaka one of these days, omitting the lamb so Celestial could eat it, too.

I avoided certain topics, like why he had come to California to look up Celestial, whether he and Wendy had any children. (Did I have any half brothers or sisters? I didn't want to know.) And I had to give him credit — he didn't pry into my life. Did that mean he respected my privacy or didn't care?

Thursday and Friday passed quickly, Saturday, with a flood of weekend tourists, even faster. Walter and I spent most of the day dealing with a steady stream of customers at the pumps.

During a brief afternoon lull, I sat down on the cement and leaned my back against the office wall. My neck and shoulders ached. I could smell gasoline on my hands, my arms, my knees. Walter handed me a Coke.

"When are you going back to Michigan?" I asked.

I'd been thinking about it all day. He'd been my father in the flesh for less than a week and already I was becoming dependent on him and hating my weakness. Well, as soon as Turbo returned, I wouldn't need Walter at the station anymore. "I mean, don't you have a job or something?"

"I guess you might say that." He stretched the skin on his forehead, but his wrinkles popped right back as soon as he let go. "Wendy and I own a shoe store called Walkabout. You've heard of the long treks the Australian aborigines take to prove their manhood?" He sat down beside me. "Our store used to be in town, next to the old Midwest Savings building. Then the whole downtown section started going downhill because of all the General Motors layoffs, so we moved out to a mall in the suburbs. It's not easy to think about the

Australian outback when you're stuck between a pizza parlor and a computer software outlet."

"I thought you were an accountant."

"When Celestial and I met, I was a junior C.P.A. with Standard Oil. I really hated that job."

"And you like selling shoes?"

"Yes, I do. 'You spend nine tenths of your life in shoes or on a mattress,' my father used to say. 'Buy the best of both.' We don't carry any junk. Started out with Clark desert boots and Hush Puppies, then moved into hiking boots. Now it's all athletic wear — aerobic shoes, court shoes, walking and running shoes, cross-trainers. Nikes, Reeboks, New Balance, Mazuno. What size do you wear? — about an eight? I'll send you —"

He stopped as a car pulled up. While he pumped five bucks of regular and rang up the sale, I picked at a loose thread on my discount tennies.

Walter's shadow fell beside my feet. "In any event, I do have to go home soon, before my employees figure they can do without me and stage a coup. I'd like to see your boss back in action, though, before I leave. And I'd like to resolve a few personal items, too."

"Such as?"

"Such as the relationship between you and me."

"Oh." I rose from the cement and walked inside.

"Tee, don't you have anything to say?" he asked from the doorway.

I pictured him driving his rental car over the mountain, getting on an airplane and flying back to Saginaw where Wendy Wife would be waiting with open arms to greet him. I pictured a bunch of kids there, too. Kids in Reeboks who weren't personal items to be resolved. I pushed in the sides of my Coke can, folded it in half and tossed it into a dirty fifty-gallon drum.

"I can buy my own shoes."

Turbo called from the hospital just before closing. "If I suspected you were even thinking of opening up tomorrow instead of taking the day off, I'd be out of here faster than a frigging Ferrari and you'd be out of the biggest candyass job of your life. Let me talk to your father." I handed the phone to Walter and watched him laugh and nod his balding head.

When he got off the phone, he hung the CLOSED sign on the door and said, "I thought you and I might do something fun tomorrow, just the two of us."

"Is this your brilliant idea or Turbo's?" I locked the cash in a safe behind the desk.

"Turbo's orders to close the station. My idea to get out of town. Unless you have other plans. Skeg works tomorrow, doesn't he? And I don't think Celestial would mind if we took off for the day. We could go roller skating in Golden Gate Park or catch a game at Candlestick. Or, if you'd prefer, we could drive up the coast and have brunch someplace on the water. What do you say?"

A picture from a long time ago popped into my brain. "Maybe we could go fishing?"

The air was still, the lagoon slick as a polished windshield. Walter pulled over near the old abandoned landfill. A great blue heron, wading knee-deep in the glassy water, stared intently at a clump of tule grass. We watched from the car as the bird suddenly whipped his head forward and stabbed at his reflection. When he emerged from the splintered water, a small silver fish wriggled in his beak. He juggled the fish lengthwise and swallowed it whole, stretching and recoiling his long neck as the ripples in the water stretched toward shore.

Then Walter accidentally leaned on the horn. The heron, with great unfurling wings, pried his twiggy legs from the lagoon and lifted into the sky, circled over the car and disappeared behind a grove of cypress trees. Walter looked at me and grinned, then jumped out of the car.

Like a magician pulling pigeons from a hat, he began pulling all sorts of stuff from the trunk of the brown Caddie.

"*Chère mademoiselle,* allow me to show you the very latest in patio furnishings." Out came a decrepit sand chair and an old ratty tatami mat that I knew had been under our house for at least two years. *"Voilà! C'est une pièce de résistance, n'est-ce pas?"* he continued, struggling to unfold the stubborn chair whose wooden arms had swollen in the dampness. At last he set the chair on the edge of a small embankment above the water, then spread the moldy grass mat beside it. "Ah, thees rug must have belonged to *Monsieur Pasteur, n'est-ce pas?* Part of hees, how do you say it, laboratory equeepment?"

His French accent was even worse than mine. I shook my head from side to side, giggling.

"Don't you dare laugh — it's been twenty-five years since I studied French. Now, I mean *maintenant, les, les* poles *des poissons.*" The poles of the fish? He pulled some black sticks — *les* poles *des poissons* — from the trunk and handed them to me. Two of the sticks had reels on them that were dented and scratched, slippery with fresh oil.

"*Et finalement, les, les — l'et cetera.*" On Pasteur's mat he tossed a package of hooks, some dull gray metal balls, a tube of sunscreen, a large butcher knife from our kitchen and a small jackknife from his pocket, a box of plastic garbage bags, and a package of frozen squid.

"*Une minute,*" he said as I started toward the water. "You cannot catch *les grands poissons sans un grand chapeau. Voici.*" He lifted an old rag from the trunk — a smelly canvas hat — and pulled it over my hair, then stood back to admire the effect. "Thees ees the very latest in *haute couture de Paris. C'est très chic.*" He pulled a Detroit Tigers cap over his own balding head, sashayed daintily over to the rest of the stuff, sat down

70

in the sand chair and covered his eyes with his forearm, moaning. "*Ooh-la-la. Je suis très fatigué. Et très* hung over."

By this time I was laughing so hard I nearly wet my pants. I dropped the poles in his lap and dragged the ice chest from the back seat.

"Almost like fishing for cohoe in the Great Lakes," he said, fitting together the pieces of poles. He showed me how to rig my pole with a weight, a hook, and what he called a leader, how to bait the hook with a chunk of half-frozen squid, how to cast the line into the water. He'd ferreted the secret location and proper bait for lagoon fishing from an old man at the Sand Bar who lent him the gear. "Cost me five beers, but this is guaranteed to be the hottest spot for shark on the West Coast."

"Shark?"

"Great fish, according to that old geezer. Fantastic fighters. Good eating."

"I hate sharks."

"Has anyone you know ever been attacked by a shark? Had a shark for dinner? Had dinner with a shark? Have you ever really gotten to know a shark? Have you even seen a shark close up?"

I had to admit that, no, I hadn't, except at the Academy of Sciences in the city, where they swam around in a huge circular tank. I did know how surfers felt about eating shark meat — in the great scheme of

71

the cosmos, feasting on shark was taboo if you wanted to continue to swim in shark territory with two intact arms and legs.

"What do I do if I get a bite?" I wanted to be prepared to face the menace when it came.

"Let him get a good mouth on the bait, then jerk your pole back to set the hook, like this, and reel him in."

I could picture the fish fighting really hard, could imagine Walter standing behind me, his chest supporting my back, his arms around my waist as I reeled in this great monster of a shark. The yearning wasn't so very different from the desire I felt for Skeg's body, and, suddenly, I was ashamed and angry. How could I want this strange man, this balding joker, to hold me? I squinted against the sun and made a lousy cast.

The sun warmed my head, even through the funny hat Walter had given me, and reflected off the water onto my face. I knew I should rub some sunscreen on my nose and bare arms, but I didn't want to put my pole down. There was something hypnotic about watching the line disappear into the water, watching the water glide by the line as it flowed in from the ocean and began to fill up the lagoon. I didn't want to break the spell.

Walter tossed his line way out, a hundred feet from shore, with an easy, graceful movement of his shoulder, arm, and wrist. I watched him carefully, then reeled in my line and tried again. My baited hook plunked directly into the water ten feet away. He didn't laugh and didn't stand behind me or put his hand over mine on ι'.e pole and show me how to do it better. "It just takes a little practice," he said softly.

Having a father took practice, too.

The incoming tide covered the mud flats. The water, rippled now by a light breeze, lapped the sand at our feet. A few harbor seals drifted by, on their way from Pickleweed Island to the open ocean. A flock of ducks settled a few hundred yards out.

"Mallards?" Walter asked, gesturing with the tip of his pole.

"Pintails, mostly. See how their tail feathers stick up when they feed? And the white curves on the sides of their necks? But there are mallards over there in the cove, and a few mud hens, too." I pointed to the marshy area where a tiny stream emptied into the lagoon.

"How did you learn so much about birds?"

"One of Serenity's boyfriends was an ornithologist."

"Ah. Serenity. The painter, right? Whatever happened to her?"

I told him about Serenity's sudden departure from Harmony House, then about Rose and Monarch's conversion to the Rajneesh.

"So that's when you and Celestial moved to the cottage?"

I nodded. And that's when Celestial moved into another dimension. I wondered, not for the first time, if the cottage had done something to Celestial's mind. Was it haunted by a ghost called Astraeus? If we were to move now, perhaps her connection to the creepy intruder would be broken. Maybe Walter would change his mind and stay in Arena. We could rent a big house for the three of us. I snorted.

"What's so funny?"

"Nothing." I reeled in my hook and cast it out again, the line zinging over my head as it flew toward the feeding pintails. The baited hook and weight landed in the water with a splash that sent the ducks scurrying into the air. "What kind of house do you and Wendy live in?"

"It's a great place — an old farmhouse with thick stone walls. Two stories. There's a covered porch in front with a big bench swing, a huge apple tree in back, a cistern in the basement. The neighborhood's so crowded now you'd never guess it used to be farm country. The old apple tree is all that's left of the original orchard. It must have been a beautiful farm once. A beautiful town, for that matter, before all the factories were built and the trees cut down and the river polluted."

"Why do you stay, if it's changed so much?"

"Good question." He scratched the stubble on his

chin. "Well, my business is there. It would be difficult to start over somewhere else. And the people are friendly and unpretentious and help their neighbors in times of trouble." Did his voice shake when he said that? He cleared his throat. "Of course, Saginaw can't hold a candle to this area in terms of dramatic, physical beauty," he added.

"Did Wendy grow up there, too? Did you know each other when you were kids?" I bit my lip. Why had I asked that?

"I first ran into Wendy, you might say, at Old South School." He leaned back and grinned. "One day Billy Schneider, the fastest, toughest kid in the fourth grade, challenged me to a race. He bet his 'fifty-nine Mickey Mantle against my 'fifty-five Sandy Koufax — baseball cards, you know? — that I couldn't beat him to the back door of the school with a thirty-foot head start. I wanted that Mantle so badly I could taste the bubble gum it had come with. I thought if I really concentrated all my energy into each step, like Mantle clearing second on a long drive to right field, I just might win. So I put my head down and charged toward the back door of the school. The next thing I knew, I'd plowed smack into some obstacle. When my head stopped spinning, I saw a girl in a blue jacket, doubled over, gasping for breath. I was furious. In those days I didn't even speak to girls. This one had stepped right in my way and cost me the most valuable card in my collection. She deserved to have more than the wind knocked out of her. When Billy Schneider strutted back from the finish line to collect, I punched him in the gut. Miss Braun, the principal, suspended me for three days."

He chuckled, opened a beer from the cooler, and passed it to me. I took a swig and handed it back.

"Wendy was a year behind me. I saw her every once in a while from a distance. Then her family moved across town, and we went to different junior highs. I forgot all about her. One evening during my senior year of high school, I tripped over a pair of feet in the bleachers at a basketball game and fell in her lap. 'Well, if it isn't Mickey Mantle,' she said."

He took a long drink of beer, then settled back in his chair and continued. "We dated off and on that year and the following summer. Then I went off to college in East Lansing. Wendy finished high school and attended secretarial school in Detroit. We didn't see each other again until the week before I left for Vietnam. I ran into her, figuratively this time, at a local bar. We had a few drinks together and she promised to keep in touch. She wrote to me with all the gossip from Saginaw. I wrote back with all the news from Saigon. When I got my discharge, I returned to Michigan and fell right in with her circle of friends, all of whom I knew from Wendy's letters. Six months later we married."

So that's why he didn't come back to Arena, to Celestial.

"You know, I saw one of those Mantle cards for sale at a flea market last year for two hundred and fifty dollars."

"Tell me about your friends. I haven't met any but Skeg. Who else do you hang out with?"

"Well, there's Turbo. I consider him one of my best friends, even though he's my boss. We talk about everything — town politics, different weights of oil, spark plug brands, you know, important stuff." I liked making Walter smile. "I know tons of people at school, but I don't really have a lot in common with most of the people in my classes." Many of them seemed young to me.

"Don't you have a best friend your age? A girl?"

I thought a moment about that, both the question and the fact that he seemed genuinely interested in me, in a curiously chauvinistic way. "Don't you think a girl can have a best friend who isn't a girl?" I asked him.

"Of course I do. I just meant that it would be nice for you to have someone your own age and sex to talk with and do things with. You know, like playing with dolls and taking ballet lessons and all those girl things."

The side of his mouth twitched into a grin.

I reeled in my line and made another cast, this time almost as far as Walter's. "I used to have a best friend, a girl my age whose mother was a hairdresser. Sasha taught me how to tease my hair and curl my eyelashes and stuff Kleenex in my training bra and all those girl things."

Walter roared at that, so I told him all about Sasha, about how we had been best pals since kindergarten, despite the radical differences in our mothers' lifestyles and hairstyles and nail styles. Then I told him how Sasha's mother had remarried a rich real estate broker and moved to Atlanta when we were fourteen. Sasha had written page after page of letters about her private school, about the debutante parties she attended, the English riding lessons, the formal teas. The last letter I'd received from her a few months back described the dry-out clinic for teenage alcoholics she'd been sent to after her abortion.

"If that's what happens when you go over the mountain and into the real world," I said, slowly reeling in my line, "I think I'll stay in Arena Beach with my old inappropriate friends."

We propped our poles against pieces of driftwood and anchored the handles in the sand, then settled down to lunch. Walter's line twitched a few times, but I didn't get a nibble.

"I think I've gained five pounds this week," he said, sipping on a beer and patting the paunch that pushed his T-shirt over the waistband of his shorts. "What was in that frittata?"

"Artichoke hearts, eggs, cheese, and jalapeños."

"Mm. You didn't learn to cook from your mother?"

"No way, José." I lay back on the mat and closed my eyes against the sun. "Did you ever think about Celestial, after you and Wendy got married?"

"Well, your mother certainly has a way of haunting the imagina —"

Just then my pole leaped from its hole and sped across the sand. Walter lurched from his chair and tackled it. "Suffering succotash! Grab this thing, will you?"

I jumped up and took the pole from his hands. The line slipped off the reel in great coils. I shoved the butt of the pole against my thigh and turned the handle, clicking the bail over. The tip of my pole curved toward the bottom of the lagoon as the prehistoric monster at the end of the line raced for the channel that led to the open ocean and freedom.

I reeled and reeled till my fingers were ready to fall off. My wrist and forearm ached and my thigh felt like a pestled mortar. I could see the shark's dorsal fin break the surface, see its wake as I dragged it slowly toward me. Its tail thrashed the water and scattered a fountain of glassy shards in the air.

"That's it," Walter kept saying over and over. "Nice and steady, that's it. You're doing great."

Suddenly there it was, just below our feet, writhing and slamming its body into the muddy bottom, churning up great clouds of silt. "We don't have a net!" Walter called as he jumped into the water, grabbed the shark by the tail, and tossed it toward the shore. When the fish hit the bank, my line snapped. Walter lunged after the wily beast, snatched it once again, and hurled it into the air. It landed with a thud right beside my feet.

The four-foot-long shark had gray and tan mottled sides and a smooth pearly belly. Even though its evil mouth revealed rows of sharp teeth, it seemed pitifully defenseless now. Walter splashed out of the water, grabbed the piece of driftwood my pole had been leaning against, and raised it over the shark's head.

"Stop!" I screamed, appalled at what he was about to do. His shorts were soaked, and dirty water streamed down his hairy legs and onto his bare feet. Slowly he lowered the club. When he wiped his sweaty forehead, he left a big streak of mud on his bald spot. I felt horrified and sick and happy and proud, all at the same time. Panting heavily, he watched me watching him. At last he reached down, grabbed the shark by the tail, and flung it back into the lagoon.

Then he turned and held up his right hand for a high five. "What a team," he said.

I slapped his hand and then he grabbed mine and pulled me toward him, gave me a wet squeeze, and yelled, "Whooie! What a woman!"

Chapter 6

When Skeg pulled into town with Turbo in the back of his bus, horn beeping, the afternoon regulars poured out of the Sand Bar and cheered. The fire siren wailed. The street dogs howled. At the stop sign, Skeg jumped out of the bus and opened the sliding door on the side. Then he jumped back in and drove around in circles in the middle of the intersection while Turbo leaned out and made obscene gestures.

Back at the station, Turbo shook everybody's hand, including Walter's, then waddled into the office and sank heavily into his desk chair.

He spent the rest of the afternoon complaining. Why did we have so many cars on the lot? Why hadn't we told the owners to pick them up, that we couldn't handle all those jobs? What made me think Chip Higgins needed a new alternator instead of a battery? Why did Walter check the customers' tires when they didn't even ask him to? Who the hell had ruined his chair by taping all the holes? He liked the goddamn holes. Then he started griping about child labor laws and the hours I'd been working. Was I trying to rip him off or hoping to get the government on his case?

I kept reminding myself that he didn't mean what he said. He'd lost fifteen pounds in the hospital and quit smoking, but he still looked terrible — yellow and exhausted. Maybe it was the drugs he was taking for his heart, or the effects of nicotine withdrawal. You'd think the end of the world was coming when I put the wrong air filter in Bob Delgado's Chevy.

"Female mechanics," he spat contemptuously. "Why the hell didn't you look up the part number in the goddamn manual?"

"I couldn't find the goddamn manual. It wasn't on the shelf with the other goddamn manuals."

"Did you look in the cabinet, genius?"

Turbo kept odd and ends, mostly unpaid bills and order forms, in one of those metal cabinets that serve as stands for five-gallon bottles of spring water. I'd never seen any water, bottled or otherwise, in the office. Now he stomped over to the cabinet, ripped open the door, and growled like a bustled muffler when the contents tumbled all over the floor.

Walter poked his head in the door. "Everything all right in here?"

I thought Turbo would bite Walter's head off, but he merely grunted.

Walter picked up the mess on the floor while I changed Bob Delgado's air filter. Then, with great tact and sincerity, Walter convinced Turbo to let him take home the books and straighten out the accounting.

He worked late into the night, long after Celestial and I went to bed, and most of the next day at the station. After closing on Tuesday, he presented the cold, hard facts. Turbo was three months behind on his rent, already stretched to his credit limit with all his parts suppliers, and losing an average of $250 a week. When Walter asked about his medical bills, all Turbo said was, "Goddamn vultures."

"I can keep working full time," I offered. "I don't have to finish school this semester."

"You think your mother would ever forgive me if I encouraged you to drop out two months short of graduation?"

"Celestial wouldn't care. And you're the one who's always saying a high school diploma isn't worth —"

"Piss off, Tee," he said in a surprisingly weak voice that made me want to cry.

"You know," Walter said gently, "you'd probably pick up a lot more local business if you cleaned up this dump."

Turbo glowered at us both from his mended chair, then swept everything off the top of his desk and onto the filthy floor with one swipe of his thick arm. "You want to clean it up? Be my guest."

*   *   *

When Walter and I got home that evening, Celestial was sitting on the front steps. "I thought we could have a picnic on the mountain. Would Skeg like to come? Do you think we should bring Mao? Will ten sandwiches be enough?"

We stopped for Skeg on our way past the Lip and drove slowly up the mountain in the Whale, Skeg and me in the front, the old folks in back. Celestial kept cooing over the flowers. "I'm going to embroider a quilt with poppies and lupine and clarkia and iris, so I can wake up every morning in a bed of wildflowers." Her lupine-blue eyes sparkled in the rearview mirror. "Oh, look," she said, pointing out her window. Half a dozen deer browsed in a wide meadow. In the mirror I saw Walter lean over and put his cheek next to hers to see the animals. I gave Skeg a friendly poke in the ribs.

We chose a sunset view and spread an old blanket in the thick green grass. Celestial pulled a bottle of wine and a six-pack of Coke from the cooler. While Walter opened the wine, she passed out sandwiches — cashew butter with banana and teriyaki tofu with tomato.

After we ate, Skeg fetched a football from the Whale's trunk. Then he and Walter spread out to play catch. I felt full and happy and peaceful until I remembered Turbo and the gas station. Celestial patted my hand. "How are things going at the station? How is Turbo?" I was so upset about Turbo that I almost didn't notice her mind reading.

"The station's a mess and so is he. It'll be a miracle

if he doesn't go under." I knew exactly what miracle was required. If Walter stayed in Arena, the two of us could help Turbo together. Hadn't my father himself said we were a team? I could man the garage while he handled the finances. After all, he'd owned a business for years. A shoe store couldn't be that much different from a gas station.

A miracle. That's what it would take, all right. But miracles happened only to people who believed in them, and I'd learned long ago how foolish that was.

The football whizzed past my nose. "Sorry," Walter said as he jogged by the blanket to retrieve it. "Nice throw," he yelled to Skeg, then fired it back up the hill and moved away.

"Honey, I'm glad you've had an opportunity to meet your father and get to know him. But he has to go back to Michigan, to his other responsibilities."

"If they're so important, why hasn't he told me about all these other responsibilities?" I picked at the grass beside the blanket.

"Have you asked him?"

She rose from the blanket and strolled up the hillside. "Come count deer with me, Skeg," I heard her say.

The responsible one came over to the blanket and flopped down beside me. I rolled onto my stomach and watched the sun flatten out like a neon jelly bean over the ocean.

"Penny for them?" Walter said. What a dork.

85

"They're not worth a penny."

"Try me."

I yanked a long blade of grass from the ground and began to chew the end of it. "Do you and Wendy have any kids?"

"I thought you'd never ask."

He drew a wallet from the back pocket of his jeans and pulled out a photograph of three kids sitting on a wide swing. The big one reminded me of Goofy — tall, skinny, and dark, with ears that drooped down toward his bony shoulders. He had acne on his left cheek and looked ready to strangle the photographer. A girl sat beside him. She had curly brown hair and buck teeth and wore thick glasses. Her stomach stuck out under her striped T-shirt. She seemed pretty happy with herself. The boy on the other end of the swing was clowning for the camera. His eyes were the same brown as his messy hair. And — here's what intrigued me most of all — he had freckles, a galaxy of brown spots all over his face and arms.

The freckles on my own arms began to itch. "What are their names?"

"That's Carter, on the left. He's very bright — a computer whiz, a D and D fanatic. He plans to be an engineer, maybe work for NASA one day. He's fourteen, a freshman in high school, the family cynic. He gets very good grades, mostly A's, but still wets his bed occasionally — he's an extremely heavy sleeper.

"Melissa's the easy one. She never complains, never

worries, although Wendy says that will probably change with age. She's nine, a third grader, not an exceptional student. She's very nearsighted, had to wear an eyepatch for a year when she was in preschool, then progressed to bifocals in kindergarten. She's slated for braces next year, but even that doesn't bother her. She loves music, plays the piano. I think she's very talented for her age but, of course, I'm slightly biased." He grinned.

I decided I would get along with Melissa, but I wasn't sure about Carter. I liked computers, but I'd always hated Dungeons and Dragons — never knowing what was going to happen next, what kind of monster was waiting behind the locked door.

"What about him?" I pointed to the sunshine-and-freckles kid on the end.

"That's Owen. Fearless Owen. Owen the Omniscient." Walter took the photograph from my fingers. His hand trembled. "Owen would try anything. He never thought about getting hurt, never seemed to learn the connection between cause and effect. If I ride my unicycle down the sidewalk and juggle four oranges at the same time, then I might lose my balance and fall."

His use of the past tense didn't escape my notice. "And did he? Fall, I mean."

"He ran into a fire hydrant and smashed his elbow." Walter's voice shook. I could almost picture the boy falling off his unicycle and hitting the hydrant, oranges flying in all directions and finally rolling into the gutter.

"But he's all right now?"

Walter didn't say anything for a long time. Then he spoke so softly I almost couldn't hear. "The doctors put a pin in his arm and a cast all the way from his shoulder to his fingertips. That was a few days after Thanksgiving. Over Christmas vacation, he was messing around with a couple of his buddies by the river. The water had iced over, but they all knew enough to stay off it. Then one of the boys dared Owen to cross. He made it all the way to the other side but, when he got halfway back, the ice broke. Without the cast, he might have been able to pull himself out. As it was, he just disappeared." He stopped talking and stared at the horizon.

How would it feel, for a parent to lose a child? Much worse than a child losing a parent, I thought. Life wasn't supposed to work that way. I chewed on the tough blade of grass, not knowing what to say.

Walter put the photograph back in his wallet as Celestial and Skeg came over the ridge. Then we all watched the colors fade from the sky while Celestial raved on about the deer.

Walter began the cleanup early the next day. "I woke up a few hours ago and couldn't get back to sleep," he said when I arrived at the station at 6:30. "Figured I might as well be doing something useful."

He had moved everything off the shelves and floor of the office, stashed it all in boxes outside the door. Early morning light poured in the clean front windows.

I could already see some potential. "Maybe Turbo could put in a soda machine and a rack for candy and chips and stuff like that," I said.

"Great idea. Once we get rid of all the junk, there'll be plenty of space. But to generate the kind of cash flow he needs, he should hire a full-time mechanic. He ought to carry more tires, too. And lower his gas prices. The tourists might pay anything, but the locals won't."

By the time Turbo showed up around nine, Walter had scrubbed the walls and begun to mop the floor. Turbo tracked water around the office, scowling and grumbling. Walter politely suggested he wait on his customers.

I managed to replace a water pump and a fan and do two oil changes while Turbo pumped gas and complained about how slow and stupid I was. After a humongous lunch at the Snack Shack he seemed to feel better. He even helped Walter clear off the workbench in the shop.

Before long, he and Walter were sorting and cleaning tools and swapping war stories. Turbo told a few whoppers about the motorcycle gang he used to ride with. Walter told about basic training and the army and Vietnam. To hear him talk, you'd think the war was one big joke. Was that the only way he could bear to talk about it?

"Fourteen-twelve," Larry called from the serving line behind me.

We were playing informal beach volleyball with a bunch of the locals — Gus and Larry, a couple of the lifeguards and their girlfriends, Bill Stuart, the owner of the Snack Shack, and his wife, Julie. I grinned at Skeg through the net. The sun had gone down and we were trying to finish the game while we could still see.

The ball flew over my head toward the center of the opposite side. Bill bumped it high into the air, then blasted it across the net toward me. I dove for it and missed, but Gus managed to return it across the net again. Bill leaped for it and swung but knocked the ball into a wobbly vertical spin. Skeg lunged for it to give it an extra boost, but he tripped in the sand and fell. Julie bumped the ball over the net. It floundered erratically toward my head. I jumped up and slammed it right past Skeg's nose.

"Game!" Larry shouted, giving me a congratulatory punch in the arm. "Nice goin', Tee."

Skeg slipped under the net, smiling broadly. "I'll say." As everyone began to disperse, Skeg slid his arm around my shoulder and headed toward the parking lot, the volleyball under his other arm.

"Say, Tee, where'd you learn to spike like that?" Bill asked as he and Julie passed us near Skeg's bus.

"She gets a lot of practice fighting off lecherous surfers," Skeg said, grinning sideways at me.

Julie chuckled. "I don't blame her."

"Well, stay cool guys," Bill said as they disappeared into the night shadows.

"'Night, Bill. 'Night, Julie."

"See ya," Skeg called after them. He tossed the leather ball into the back of his bus, hopped in himself, then gave me a hand up, pulling me onto a beach towel on the floor in one move.

"You get so . . . intense . . . when you . . . play," he said, kissing me between words. "It's really . . . sexy."

I kissed him back. "You're not so . . . bad . . . yourself," I replied breathlessly.

Before long, we were rolling around on the floor of the bus, getting all tangled up and involved. Then my left ankle snagged a leash line and a surfboard fell onto Skeg's back.

"Saved by the board," I said, smothering a giggle.

He propped himself up on one elbow and rubbed his shoulder. "I knew I should have put that thing away earlier," he said ruefully. He shook his head and knocked his temple with his palm, as if to clear water from his ears. "So tell me one of those war stories that Walter told you today," he said out of the blue.

Was he trying to get his mind off his hormones or

thinking of joining the army? I didn't know, but I appreciated his tactics and was relieved to have some breathing space. I sat up, pulled my sweatshirt back down over my jeans, and leaned my back against the seat. "He told Turbo, not me."

"I bet you listened, though."

"Well," I stalled, embarrassed. "I did, but I still can't tell you. I've never been good at telling stories. You know how some people can remember every joke they've ever heard and others can't? Well, I can't." How else could I divert his attention? "Why don't you tell me a story?"

He flopped over and put his head in my lap.

"Why won't you make love with me?"

If I could see his eyes, I knew they'd pull me in. I chewed on a ragged hangnail. "I guess I'm afraid."

"Of getting pregnant? We can take care of that, you know." He pulled my hand away from my face and kissed my fingertips ever so gently.

"I know. It's just . . . Oh, I don't know. I suppose I believe that having sex, making love, is a commitment, and I don't think I'm ready for that."

"Why not?"

"My life is too confusing already. I don't want things to change. I just want everything to stay the way it is, the way it was before my father came and messed things up. Everything was so much clearer before."

"That's the first time I've heard you call him that."

"What?"

"Your father."

Skeg drove me home, but he didn't get out of the bus. He leaned his chin on the steering wheel and stared out the window. "I know I promised I wouldn't pressure you, babe. To do anything you're not ready to do. But sometimes I can't help myself. I just go crazy with wanting you."

I felt like a little kid with a learning disability. Skeg was my very patient, very understanding teacher. I swallowed, not knowing what to say.

"Do me a favor?" he asked.

"Sure."

"Let me know if you change your mind?"

I grinned. "You'll be the first to hear."

Chapter 7

Celestial sat on the back porch, staring at the tangle of weeds and wildflowers that served as our garden. Was she having a conversation with Astraeus? No, thank goodness. As soon as she heard me, she smiled brightly. "Good morning, sleepyhead."

"What time is it?" I asked groggily.

"Almost nine. Walter said he and Turbo could manage at the station this morning. You slept right through your alarm, so we both assumed you needed the extra rest. Would you like me to fix you some breakfast? A boiled egg? Tea? Toast?"

"Thanks. I'll just have a bowl of cereal." I stretched. Nine o'clock! Had I really slept for ten hours?

As I dressed, I thought about Carter and Melissa. Maybe they could come to Arena, if Wendy Wife would permit them to visit her husband's illegitimate child and ex-lover. A brother and sister. What would I do with them? I could teach Melissa to make pasta and do a tune-up. Celestial could sew a dress or bead a sweatshirt for her. Carter sounded far too cerebral for me. Maybe Turbo could talk computers and astrophysics with him.

I'd rather take Owen hunting for buried treasure on the beach. Skeg could teach him to surf. If Owen could ride a unicycle, he'd be a natural at surfing. I could show him the hang glider launching sites on the mountain and, when he got old enough, even buy him a lesson. Fearless Owen. Maybe he could teach me not to be afraid of heights.

I poured myself a bowl of cereal, remembering the impish look on Owen's face in the snapshot Walter had shown me. Omniscient Owen. Somehow he seemed more real to me than the two who were still alive.

Celestial set a mason jar of wildflowers on the table, then returned with a mug of tea. "Owen looked very much like you. He had your freckles," she said, sitting down opposite me. "But I do believe Melissa has your nose. Carter must look like his mother."

I almost choked on my cornflakes but, before I had a chance to protest her telepathic snooping, she smiled and asked if she could ride down the hill with me. She wanted to help with the renovation of the station.

A red Chevette with a dangling front bumper, crumpled hood, and smashed windshield occupied my usual parking space. I pulled in behind it and read the bumper stickers: GUN CONTROL = GOVN'T CONTROL and FIGHT FOR YOUR RIGHT TO BEAR ARMS. I could hardly wait to meet the driver.

Turbo was hosing down the pavement. Dirty water, clouded with ribbons of oil, swirled around the tires of the Chevette. "Whose car?" I asked.

"Some jackass who got loaded and went off the coast road last night. Got stuck on a boulder a few yards over the edge, the only thing between him and a three-hundred-foot drop-off. Facial cuts and a broken collarbone, according to Gus."

I noticed the HELP WANTED sign in the window. So Turbo was going to take Walter's advice and hire a new mechanic. Did that mean I wouldn't have a job? Maybe Celestial could take her psychic skills to Las Vegas and win enough money to pay our rent next month.

"Well, sleeping beauty, are you going to stand around all day and watch the rest of us work our butts off?" Turbo said.

I hustled into the shop.

While Turbo helped me with a brake job, Celestial and Walter began to transform the jaundiced exterior walls. From the shop I could hear Walter's humming, then Celestial's soprano, then their two voices blending. Some of the songs I remembered from Harmony House, songs that Celestial and Serenity used to sing over their chores. *Swing Low, Sweet Chariot* and

You Are My Sunshine. This Land Is Your Land. The one with the "valdaree, valdarah-ha-ha" chorus. Unable to carry a tune myself, I appreciated how the lines tumbled over one another and came together at the end, like two trails splitting and meeting again. I could almost picture Serenity and Celestial singing on the mountain, could vaguely recall riding in a backpack as they hiked and harmonized.

"Needs new calipers, too. See how shot the old ones are?" Turbo said, snapping me from my dream.

When the bell dinged, I went outside to wait on a customer. Ten bucks of supreme? Be happy to check the oil. It's down half a quart. You'll add it yourself at home? Fine. I'll get your change. You're welcome. Come again.

The car pulled out and I wandered around to the back of the building. Celestial perched two thirds of the way up a metal ladder like a dainty tropical bird. She was painting the trim red under the overhang. In his Tigers cap and new surfer pants, Walter was rolling white paint in broad swaths across the stucco walls.

I leaned against the corner of the building and listened to them sing.

I gave my love a cherry that had no stone.
I gave my love a chicken that had no bone.
I gave my love a story that had no end.
I gave my love a baby with no cryin'.

Clear as a raindrop I remembered Celestial singing to me as I fell asleep on my mattress under the eaves in the attic of Harmony House. Although the words were riddles and the music incredibly sad, I always felt very safe and peaceful when she sang to me. The riddles, I knew, would be answered in the last verse, if I could only stay awake that long. A cherry in blossom has no stone. A chicken in the egg has no bone. A story in the telling has no end. And a baby when it's sleeping doesn't cry.

Now it struck me that all the riddle answers were images of events stuck in time, suspended, unfinished. A blossom, an egg, a story, a sleeping baby. All of them eventually changed, grew, ended.

The white paint Walter was spreading on the gas station wall was so bright in the sunlight that it made my eyes water.

Skeg and I walked along the beach in the dark while the waves broke in phosphorescent bands nearby. The glow came from billions of microorganisms in the water that sometimes floated in with the tide. I thought about how wonderfully adaptable those tiny creatures must be, to survive such a pounding. Were they covered with shell-like armor or did their strength come from soft, fluid bodies that conformed to the molecular structure of salt water? Why did they appear so infrequently? What happened to them after they washed up on the beach? I knew the answers to my questions must be in some marine biology textbook. For an instant I was almost sorry I hadn't applied to college.

Skeg scrambled like a monkey up one of the lifeguard towers and looked out to sea.

"How's the view?" I asked from below.

"Epic. Climb up and see."

I wrapped my arms around my chest and stared at the waves. "You know I can't handle heights."

He jumped to the sand behind me, put his hands on my shoulders, and nibbled my ear. "Soft as shark skin," he whispered.

"Do you really believe a shark could smell shark meat on your breath, could tell if you ate one of its brothers or sisters?" I asked.

He nuzzled my neck. "No, but I think you could. If I ever ate any." He turned me toward him and kissed my eyelids and pulled my eyebrows with his lips.

"Let's walk," I said, skipping a few yards ahead.

He caught up with me and slipped an arm around my waist. "Did I tell you that Billabong wants me to surf for them?"

I kept walking. The wind made a rushing sound in my ears. "What do you mean?"

"They pay me to surf, I wear their gear."

I stopped dead in my tracks. "They'll *pay* you to surf?"

"They do it all the time. Some people — present company excepted — actually think surfers are cool and want to copy them, so companies like Billabong hire dudes like me to advertise their products. A couple guys I know make ten times more money on endorsements than they do in prizes." Even in the darkness I could see a scowl cross his face. "You don't think it's a sellout, do you? I mean, even a surfer has to earn a living."

I gave his question serious consideration. "No, I don't think it's a sellout, not if you really like their stuff."

I shoved my hands into the pockets of my jeans and shivered.

"Cold?" Skeg asked. I nodded.

He pulled me close and I could feel his warmth under his jacket and through our respective sweatshirts. I watched the silver-tipped waves over his shoulder and jumped a little as an icy tongue of water raced up the sand and licked my bare feet. He walked me backwards to dry ground, then rubbed my back briskly up and down. "You're freezing, aren't you?" He took my icy hands, pulled them under his shirt, and warmed them in his armpits.

"Better?"

"Much. Thanks." I sat down on the sand and hugged my knees. Skeg plunked down beside me, then leaned forward and pulled something from his back pocket.

"I almost forgot. I found something on the beach this morning. I saved it for you."

Curious, I reached for his closed fist. "What is it?"

"Close your eyes."

I closed them. He took my hand and pressed something into my palm.

"Guess what it is."

The object was hard and dry and a bit bumpy, flattish, circular, about the size of a silver dollar.

"A large button?"

"Much more valuable than that."

"A Spanish doubloon?"

"Closer, but not right. It's older, a lot older."

"Um, a beach agate?"

"Go ahead and look," he said eagerly.

I opened my eyes and held the disc up to the faint light from the stars. It was a fossilized sand dollar, probably millions of years old. Bits and pieces of them washed down from the cliffs to the north from time to time and came in with the tide. I turned it over and traced the faint, star-shaped pattern on the other side.

"It's the most perfectly shaped one I've ever seen," I said, my fingers tingling with the unexpected sweetness of the gift.

I gave my love a cherry . . .

When Skeg leaned forward and kissed me gently, I felt the warmth from my fingertips crawl up my arm and slowly spread all through my body. My insides were like jellyfish. I wished I had something to give him in return for the sand dollar.

I gave my love a story that has no end.

Then and there I made a decision, but it took me a few minutes to break off our kiss. "Remember last night when you asked me to tell you if I changed my mind?" It seemed as though years had passed since then. "Well, I think I changed it. Or it changed. Or something."

Skeg stopped breathing and stared at me. The waves spread in radiant beams behind his head. His hair was white in the starlight. He looked like a little kid, like Saint-Exupéry's Little Prince alone on the desert. Sharp grains of sand cut into my ankles. The waves sent tiny earthquakes up my legs.

I reached into my pocket and pulled out the foil package I'd been keeping there for a while, just in case. "So how do I put this on you?"

He looked down at the wrapped condom and blushed. "You really want to know?"

I handed him the package. "Show me."

Celestial and Walter weren't home, I discovered to my great relief when Skeg dropped me off. He'd been so sweet, so understanding when I told him I wanted to sleep at home, in my own bed.

I stepped into the shower and rinsed the sand off my arms and legs, from between my toes and other, more intimate crevices, wondering about the whole act of love. My new, nonvirginal body didn't feel any different from the old one. Had I changed in any permanent way? I didn't think so. This whole sex thing seemed highly overrated. Or maybe it was an acquired taste, like sushi or dark beer? The best part of making love had been the look of surprise in Skeg's eyes when I told him I'd changed my mind. The next best part was the calm feeling afterwards, but that had been interrupted by a chunk of Styrofoam that tumbled down the beach and blew into the side of my head.

I dried off and slipped into an old flannel nightgown, then wiped a patch of condensation from the mirror. I didn't look any different.

But as I stared at my reflection, I remembered another mysterious sensation I'd had on the beach, a feeling of stepping outside myself and watching from a distance. I was riding the waves with the tiny animals, cresting and falling, cresting and falling, and finally being lifted up and then thrown down on the sand, pushed toward the houses that lined the beach, toward Skeg, toward myself, toward darkness. I didn't think this was orgasm, because it wasn't connected with anything Skeg was doing at the time. And I hadn't particularly enjoyed it. I didn't like losing control like that.

As the mirror clouded over again, I watched my face slowly disappear.

Chapter 8

"I am Astraeus," Celestial said in the voice that sounded like a cross between Mahatma Gandhi and Dylan Thomas. I'd gotten up to get a glass of water but stopped dead in my tracks at my half-open door when I heard her. In the candlelit living room, I could see the back of Walter's head over the top of the wing-back and Celestial's slippered feet at the end of the couch. "I am from a place and time beyond and encompassing this place and time. Why have you called me here?"

I pulled the door shut. How dare she! Celestial had sworn she'd never channel while I was in the house.

The first time I'd intentionally watched her do it — request Astraeus's presence for someone who wanted to ask him questions — I sat on a pillow at her feet with the permission of Mrs. Dunn, an old lady who lived up the street from us. Mrs. Dunn's husband had

104

drowned twenty years before in a boating accident. She wanted to know if he'd forgiven her for nagging him. She had barely begun to explain which Mr. Dunn she was asking about — Mr. John Thomas Dunn, born in Oakland in 1901 — when I looked up at my mother's face. Celestial's head had dropped to one side. Her eyes had rolled back in their sockets. All I could see were two slim crescents of white beneath her half-closed lids. As her mouth formed the words, "Bring them up, Mrs. John Thomas Dunn, bring up all your worries," I brought up a lunch of noodle soup and orange slices. Mrs. Dunn dabbed a handkerchief at the mess on my lap while Celestial continued in that nauseating voice. "Cleanse your soul of worry and guilt, Mrs. Dunn. Worry and guilt are products of your earthly mind." I knew my mother believed I manufactured enough worry to make myself vomit, that the mess on my lap was a product of my earthly mind. But this crazy act of hers was what made me sick. Didn't she understand?

The second and last time I'd witnessed her voodoo routine had been one day, a year or so ago, when I stayed home from school with a sore throat. Her scheduled clients were an infertile couple from Berkeley. She'd been unable to reach them to cancel. The man, a lawyer who'd heard about my mother from a San Quentin parolee Celestial had once advised, wanted to discuss the ethics of surrogate motherhood with Astraeus. The woman sought counsel on artificial insemination. Despite my better judgment, I eavesdropped from my bed. I even wondered whether Celestial/Astraeus might have some worthwhile advice for these frustrated people. But as soon as Celestial — my mother?! — began to speak in that strange voice, I heard the blood pounding at my temples. My swollen tonsils pressed against my eardrums. I closed my eyes and took long, ragged breaths, convinced I'd suffocate before anyone found me. By the time the couple left and Celestial came into my room, my throat hurt so much I couldn't even speak. Sweat poured off my body. Celestial bathed my arms and back and face with a cool washcloth dipped in geranium water and promised never again to channel while I was home.

Some promise.

Walter cleared his throat. Through the crack between my door and the warped jamb, I could see him resettle that long lock of hair over his skull.

"Celestial, I don't think, uh, I don't think I can do this."

"Celestial cannot hear you," the voice said. "She is not with us right now. Do you wish to speak with me?"

Silence. I waited, cringing inside. Did Celestial know I was listening?

"Well, I'm not sure how to talk to you. I'm not even sure I believe I am talking to anyone other than Celestial."

My sentiments exactly. In fact, when I'd analyzed

these channeling sessions, I'd come to the conclusion that Celestial was tapping a part of her subconscious that longed to give advice, to tell people what to do. Since she refused to offer opinions with her conscious mind, I could understand why she needed to disguise this side of her personality with a different voice, a different identity.

"I am not Celestial Bliss. She has graciously allowed me to use her current earthly body as a vehicle but, make no mistake, I am not Celestial. Now, if you don't need me, I will give Celestial back her body. Perhaps she can help you as well as I."

"No. Wait," Walter said. *Coward,* I thought. *Don't let her get away with this act.* But he continued. "I've already spoken to Celestial, but she didn't have any answers. She suggested I talk to you." Sweat glistened on top of Walter's cranium.

"Then I will try to exercise more patience. Speak when you are ready."

I could feel myself getting dizzy, so I leaned my head against the door and held on to the frame for balance. The wall creaked. I thought for sure Celestial (Astraeus?) would say something about spying, or that Walter would turn around and see me there. Holding my breath, I slid to the floor and put my ear to the crack.

"I want to ask you about truth," Walter said. "Is it always morally right to tell the truth, even if it will hurt someone else a great deal?"

I knew it! He was afraid to tell Wendy about me. Afraid or ashamed.

"Is the person who might be hurt in any danger from not knowing this truth?"

"Yes," Walter said after a minute, "she is in danger of diminishing herself by thinking she can protect herself from hurt." What on earth was he talking about?

"Ah, the delusion of self-protection. This is a phenomenon you have experienced yourself."

"How do you know?"

Astraeus ignored the question. "Do you care for this person?"

"I love her very much."

I was afraid of that. I'd foolishly allowed myself to hope that Walter no longer loved Wendy Wife, that he'd divorce her, and stay in Arena with me and Celestial.

I reminded myself to pay attention. Astraeus (Celestial?) was speaking again. "Love, as you know, can assist, even promote, healing."

"But I can't deliberately hurt someone I love."

"In my experience, more humans are hurt by ignorance than by truth. Hold on a moment, please, while I calculate this." There was a pause. "According to my figures, a person is ninety-six point six times more likely to be hurt by ignorance than by truth."

"I see," Walter said. Well, I didn't see.

"You have learned from personal experience,

Walter, that the greatest understanding and growth comes through hurt, have you not?"

"I'm beginning to learn that, yes."

"Do you imagine your loved one incapable of growth?"

"No, it's not that. If I tell her the truth, I know she will grow. But she'll also be so angry about what I did years ago that she may never forgive me. She could hate me for life."

"For this life, you mean?"

"Listen, this is the only life I know about."

"And is ignorance bliss?"

"I never realized spirits could be such wise guys."

"We like to think we are wise. Many of us have not entirely abandoned our senses of humor."

"Black humor, if you ask me."

"You are asking the questions, Walter." Was that a sigh of exasperation I heard? And whose sigh was it?

Silence. Then: "Am I wrong to want forgiveness?"

"What, exactly, is the meaning of 'wrong'? Are you speaking of greater and lesser good, or of evil? Every human being has the capacity for right and wrong, good and evil. Sometimes good and right require personal sacrifice. But this is another way we learn in our many incarnations."

"So you're saying that I should tell the truth, even if it means sacrificing the love of the person involved?"

"Are you sure the truth will cause a loss of love?"

"Are you, by any chance, acquainted with Socrates?"

"As a matter of fact, I did study with the great teacher in one of my past lives."

"Well, if it wouldn't be too much trouble, I'd appreciate your frank opinion on truth telling in my present life."

Go for it, Wally!

"In my humble opinion, the key is motivation. If you tell a painful truth in order to unburden yourself of guilt, then perhaps you would be wiser to remain silent. Inflicting hurt for this reason would only generate more guilt and might indeed be considered evil. But if you tell the truth because you love someone and truly desire this person's growth, then inflicting hurt would not be evil. Withholding the truth would be equivalent to withholding a gift — selfish, perhaps even immoral. This is my opinion. But you must determine what your motivation is.

"I have one last thought for you," Astraeus continued. "Is integrity absolute or relative?"

"That's exactly what I hoped you'd tell me."

"I have found it to be at least ninety-six point six percent absolute."

"Isn't that a contradiction in terms?"

"I prefer to call it an oxymoron, from the Greek words meaning 'sharp' and 'foolish.' Now, if you have no further questions at this time, I will release Celestial's body before we drain any more of her energy."

"I do have one more question."

"Yes?"

"How can I be sure what my motivation is?"

"That is, indeed, a great conundrum."

The living room was quiet. I felt sorry for Walter. If he told his wife about me, she would be terribly hurt and angry. If he didn't tell her, he'd have to carry the guilty secret for the rest of his life.

I heard him get up from the chair. When I peeked through the crack, I could see his stockinged feet beside Celestial's slippered ones at the bottom of the couch.

Mao growled when I crawled back into bed. I stroked his head, petting him back to contentment and sleep.

My thoughts rattled in my brain like a bad valve. I missed Skeg. I wished he were here beside me, petting me till I purred. I wondered if Walter and Celestial would snuggle together all night on the couch. I wondered what Astraeus looked like. Was he real? He was as indirect and ambivalent as Celestial. He asked more questions than he answered, hesitated to express opinions. But his humor and mathematical slant were totally unlike her. Was Astraeus a separate person or soul or spirit, an astral traveler? Astral. Astraeus. A name that someone who called herself Celestial Bliss might easily have invented. Was he simply a figment of Celestial's mind, as much a product of her artistic imagination as her name, her beadwork? I saw her holding a pair of earrings up to my cheek, saw myself in her lap, felt her rocking me. I felt myself in a backpack, rocking from side to side as Celestial climbed a trail on the mountain. I saw two deer leaping through a meadow of wildflowers. Celestial and Walter? Astraeus had spoken of past lives. Celestial believed in them too. I wondered if Mao were a reincarnation of something else — a mole, a frog, a centipede? What had I been? One of Descartes' students? A scullery maid? A cat? Skeg had certainly been a dolphin once upon a time, had slipped through the ocean, played in the waves. How did dolphins make love?

Chapter 9

Pegasus flew. His wings stretched toward the sun. His hooves sprang from the freshly painted letters above the office door: TURBOSERVICE.

Walter climbed down from the ladder and stepped back to admire his work. "Well, what do you think?"

Turbo stood there, rubbing his fat cheeks with his hand. "Mobil Oil might sue for copyright infringement, but who gives a damn."

"Tee?"

"Great." I went back to work. I needed to finish the tune-up on Trip Podell's Nissan before we closed for the rest of the weekend. I needed to keep my mind off the fact that Walter was leaving the next day at noon.

He came inside. *Okay, concentrate on what you're doing,* I told myself. *Replace the distributor cap, insert the screws, tighten them down. Now the air filter.*

"Are you sure you and Skeg won't come with us tonight? The belly dancers at this Egyptian restaurant are very sexy, I hear."

The thought of eating anything at all made me want to throw up on Trip Podell's radiator. "Positive. You and Celestial should have a night by yourselves, for old times' sake." Who knows, maybe it's not too late for you to fall in love again. Then what would you and Wendy Wife do, Wally?

"Will you be home later?" he asked. "I'd like to talk to you about a few things before I leave. If you could give me an hour or so this evening, I wouldn't need to wake you in the morning."

"I think I'm spending the night at Skeg's." I hadn't thought about this at all, but right now it seemed like a good idea.

He bunched his lips into a little wrinkled donut. "What about tomorrow, then? Breakfast at the Snack Shack?"

I tightened the wing nut on Trip's filter cover. "We might as well get it over with tonight."

"Celestial and I should be home by eleven. See you then?"

I wiped my hands on a dirty rag and nodded.

"If you decide you want to go to college, even in a few years, I'll do what I can to help. Meanwhile, until you turn twenty-one, I'll send you a check every month. Celestial's already told me not to worry about your usual expenses — rent, food, dental bills. But you might want to travel or enroll in the odd course. Invest in treasury bills. Buy a new car. Or a dress?"

He flashed me that silly grin of his and I couldn't help smiling back. It was impossible to be offended by his attempts to buy me off.

"I'll have to figure how much we can afford and let you know. I'm going to send the checks directly to you. Celestial has adamantly refused to accept any money for herself."

I sat with my back to the fireplace, hugging my knees and soaking up the warmth of the fire. I tried to look at Walter objectively, as if I'd just met him and didn't know we were related. He wasn't bad looking, even with his thinning hair and creased forehead. A bit too yuppified for my taste, in his navy blazer and tie, too intellectual in those glasses. He looked more like a teacher or social worker, maybe a shrink, than a shoe salesman. He was patient and had a good sense of humor — qualities that must have come in handy when waiting on picky customers with smelly feet. I could see why Celestial had fallen for him. He was so practical and down-to-earth. The old attraction of opposites.

"Would you do me a favor?" he asked. I must have been dazed by the heat of the fire. I agreed right away without first asking what the favor was. "Would you think about coming to Michigan for a visit, maybe this summer after your graduation? I'd like Wendy and the kids to meet you."

So he had decided to confess all and suffer the consequences. Would Wendy be hurt to the core or just angry when Walter told her about me? Would she scream at him or walk out in shock? Maybe she'd divorce him and he'd come back to California.

I tossed a piece of bark into the fire. It flared brightly but burned out in a minute. "When are you going to tell them about me?"

He cleared his throat. "Wendy already knows. She and I are going to explain everything to Carter and Melissa when I get home."

"You told her over the telephone?" For an instant I felt sorry for Wendy, getting news like this long distance. Then my curiosity took over, and I wanted to know all the details — how she reacted, what she thought of Walter and Celestial and me, of the idea of a stepdaughter. "When? What did she say?"

He took off his glasses and rubbed the spot between his eyes. Then he pulled a handkerchief from his pocket and polished the lenses. He settled the glasses back on his nose and blinked at me. "Tee," he said so softly I had to lean forward to hear. "Wendy has known about you for a long time. Since you were a baby, in fact. I told her about you before I asked her to marry me."

A spark flew out of the fireplace and landed beside my bare foot. I flicked it onto the brick hearth, but it left a small charred spot on the rug. What did he mean, since you were a baby?

"I'm sorry," he said. "I don't want to hurt you more than I have already, but I want you to know the truth."

Truth? I shook my head from side to side, convinced I'd heard the words wrong. He couldn't have known about me all these years. Couldn't have gone off and married someone besides my mother, had a bunch of kids, and ignored my existence. He put his hand under my chin and made me look at him. "Tee, are you listening to me?"

I wanted to slug him in the face, to crush his glasses in my bare hands, then stomp them into dust on the hearth. Instead I shoved his hand away, got up, and stumbled to the door.

The Whale's motor turned over instantly. I peeled out of the driveway and down the street.

I was halfway up the mountain before I saw his lights in my rearview mirror. He flashed his high beams on and off. "Liar!" I screamed at the mirror as I stepped on the gas.

The Whale fishtailed around the next hairpin. I regained control and accelerated for the next short straightaway, feeling the surge when the transmission kicked into passing gear. I flipped my mirror so his lights wouldn't shine in my eyes when he followed me around the turn.

A moment later I heard his tires squeal, then heard his rental car crash into something solid — the cliff, a tree? I kept going. He could sail off the road into oblivion, for all I cared.

I cut the next corner and narrowly missed a head-on with a car coming the other way. Adrenaline rushed. I made myself slow down a little.

At the junction, I decided to head up toward the peak, rather than down the other side of the mountain toward the city. A few minutes later I pulled off the road, turned the key, and punched the light switch.

I swear to God, I hoped he was dead. I hoped his stupid Cadillac had been smashed to smithereens. I hoped he'd been thrown from the car and impaled on a tree limb and would slowly bleed to death while the vultures pecked out his stupid, myopic eyes.

Gradually my heart stopped pounding. Every once in a while I spotted headlights snaking up the mountain, then disappearing down the other side. Finally a car continued up the way I'd come. I could hear an engine off and on, between outcroppings of rock. When he pulled in beside me, I saw the mangled fender, the broken headlight, an ugly dent in the passenger side, clumps of grass sticking out between the bottom of the door and the frame.

He kept his motor running, leaned his head on the steering wheel, and stared across at me. I glared back. Finally he buzzed down the window on the passenger side of his car and turned off his engine.

"Tee?"

I locked my door, turned away, and leaned my head

against the glass. "You lied," I said through gritted teeth. "You lied to me from the very beginning."

I heard his door open and shut, heard his shoes crunching gravel, then heard his voice next to my window. "Tee, can I talk to you? Will you let me explain?"

"Explain what — how you drove into town two weeks ago and pretended you didn't know me, pretended to be surprised I was your daughter?" I squeezed the steering wheel so hard I thought it would bend in my hands. "Go away, Walter."

He walked around the front of my car and tripped over something. A small electric thrill shot through me as he stumbled. Falling on his face would be too good for him; falling off a cliff would be more fitting.

He rapped on the window of the passenger door. "Tee, please let me in."

I stared straight ahead. "Give me one good reason why I should."

"Because I'm your father. Because I need to talk to you."

Big deal, I thought.

"Tee, let me tell you what happened."

"You'd just make a joke out of it, like the war stories you told Turbo."

"No, Tee, this isn't a joke."

"Really?" I drummed my fingers on the steering wheel.

"Tee," he said after a minute more, "please."

I looked at him then. He was close enough for me to

see his pleading expression, even in the darkness. His hair was all messed up and he had a bloody gash on the side of his forehead. His glasses rested crookedly on his nose. Slowly, I stretched my leg across the seat and unlocked the door with a bare toe.

He slid onto the seat and pulled the door closed. Neither of us said anything. The windows began to cloud over. The sky disappeared, then the mountain, the trees and bushes and grass. We were alone, separated from the rest of the world by the fog of our messy relationship. Walter took off his glasses and rubbed them with a dislodged shirttail. The cut on his forehead looked worse close up. Blood had dripped down and dried in the creases of his ear. The flesh above his temple was swollen and discolored.

"Tee, I never meant to hurt you."

"What makes you think I'm hurt?" He winced. I twisted the knife. "I thought you were going to tell me a story, Walter." How much help did he need? "Many . . . years . . . ago . . . ," I said, writing the words across the cloudy windshield with my finger.

Chapter 10

Walter cleared his throat. "Many years ago I met a very unusual woman. She was talented and perceptive and honest and entirely unaware of her own inner strength and beauty. I didn't understand why she put up with me, but I convinced myself that her amused tolerance was a fair return for my invested passion. For a few weeks, we played and made love and rarely talked about anything serious."

I closed my eyes. I could almost see them, holding hands and running down the beach, laughing. Was it Walter and Celestial I pictured, or me and Skeg? Both images squeezed my heart.

Walter continued. "One day I received a valentine, not from the woman I loved, but from my draft board. When I asked Celestial what I should do, she said the decision was mine alone. She didn't want to influence me. After days of my badgering, she finally told me what she thought about the war. She spoke quietly of morality and ethics and conscience, but she still refused to advise me. I wanted her to say she loved me, to beg me to stay with her. But she didn't.

"One night I got very drunk and asked her to marry me. She said she didn't love me enough, that she didn't think she would ever get married. I quit my job the next day and left the state, furious with her, not for her lack of love — I knew she couldn't help that and was too honest to pretend. I was angry because she wouldn't tell me what to do about the draft. Can you understand that?"

Of course I understood. But I wasn't going to give him the satisfaction of knowing how often I got mad at Celestial for the same thing, for not giving me more guidance, for not telling me what to do. "Go on," I said in a voice as steady and unemotional as I could make it.

"I joined the army, signed up for Officer Candidate School, and eventually went to Vietnam, as you know." My stomach tightened. I stared at the windshield. The words I'd written were almost invisible now. "When my year in country was up, I was stunned. Every single day, I'd pictured myself stepping on that silver bird, taking off and circling those never-ending rice paddies, those godforsaken jungles. When we actually headed across the South China Sea, I couldn't believe I was really getting away. It had to be a dream. Or a bad joke. The pilot would do a one-eighty any minute and head back to Saigon. Maybe some sly VC had planted a bomb in the cargo hold to get the last laugh. Talk about laughs. We all told so many crazy stories on the way home, I thought my face would fall off. And the booze. No wonder nothing seemed real."

The armrest cut into my back. I rearranged myself on the seat, careful not to touch him, and wondered about those stories told on the airplane. Were they all funny? I tried to picture Walter laughing and getting drunk with a bunch of other guys in uniform. *Young guys,* I thought. *Like Skeg.*

"We finally landed in California. Travis Air Force Base. Some of the men had managed to send telegrams, so there were a handful of over-dressed girlfriends and weepy parents waiting. But most of us just staggered off by ourselves."

I refused to feel sorry for him. "What happened then?"

"Well, I was definitely not ready to hop a transport back to the Midwest, so I caught a bus to Oakland, grabbed a cab, and told the driver to take me to the nearest hotel. All I could think of was a hot bath and clean sheets." He sighed. "The desk clerk wasn't exactly thrilled to get my business. I could barely stand up and must have reeked of cigarettes and booze. He claimed they were full up, but I made such a stink that he finally gave me a room just to get me out of his pristine lobby. I ordered a bottle of champagne from room

123

service and fell asleep in the tub before I finished a third of it. Lucky I didn't drown. I woke up later, dragged myself out of the cold water and tried to make up for a year's bad sleep.

"The next day I ordered one of everything on the breakfast menu, read the morning paper in bed, and tried to figure out my next move. I wasn't sure I ever wanted to leave the hotel. I thought about applying for a job as a night clerk. I'd had plenty of experience working nights.

"Finally I managed to get up, take another long soak in the tub, shave, and dress."

He laced his fingers together, put his hands behind his neck, and leaned back against the seat. "I started thinking about Celestial and wondered if she still lived in Arena. Would she even speak to me if I went to see her? I knew the antiwar movement was stronger than ever, but she had always been fair and reasonable. I decided to show her that war hadn't turned me into an evil monster. I wasn't a baby killer. Just a survivor."

He grinned at the windshield, but his grin looked more like a painful grimace. I shifted myself around again and watched trails of water move down the windshield like tracks of blood.

Walter cleared his throat and continued. "I put on my best uniform, out of sheer pride and stubbornness, I guess — I could have bought some civvies — rented a car, and headed for the coast. On the way I stopped to pick up a hitchhiker, a kid about your age. He started to get in the car, then took a look at my uniform, backed away and slammed the door. He didn't say a word, just spat on the side of the car. Welcome home, soldier.

"Well, by the time I got to Arena, my uniform was drenched. I'd fought in a war but was afraid to see an old girlfriend. At the stop sign I peeled off my jacket, tossed it on the front seat beside my hat. Strange, how I remember details of that day, even now. Anyhow, I swung by Harmony House and was relieved when it looked deserted. I drove halfway around the lagoon before I got up the nerve to turn around. This time I pulled into the driveway, parked, and knocked on the door. No answer. Around back I spotted one of Celestial's fancy skirts on the clothesline, so I knew she still lived there. I decided to drive to the beach and come back later.

"There was no mistaking me for a civilian — the haircut, the creased pants, the shoes. A pair of long-haired Frisbee players on the beach made some nasty comments. I found a place away from the wind and the remarks and took a little nap. When I woke up, the Frisbee throwers were gone.

"Back in the parking lot, my rental car had been decorated. I'd left the doors unlocked. The jacket to my uniform — or what was left of it after they slashed it up and urinated all over it — was stretched across the hood. On top of it sat my hat with a dead fish in it. I wanted to show those bastards just how tough a veteran was, but they were nowhere in sight.

"I was dumping my jacket in the trash when I heard someone singing *Puff the Magic Dragon*. One of Celestial's old favorites. I shouldn't have been surprised to hear her voice — after all, Arena was a very small place — but I panicked. I ducked behind the garbage can and watched her walk by without looking my way. On her back, a small child rode in a blue canvas pack. I couldn't tell if it was a boy or a girl, or even how old it was. I hadn't had much experience with babies. The child turned and stretched a hand in my direction."

"That was me," I said, my voice squeaky. I'd been listening so intently to Walter that I'd almost forgotten this story was about me. Now a huge lump grew in my throat.

"Yes. And when you smiled, you looked just like my mother, your grandmother. Your hair was even the same honey blond color hers used to be before it turned gray."

My grandmother? "My hair isn't blond."

"It was then."

I twisted a strand of brown hair around my finger, remembering a portrait of me on the living room wall at Harmony House. Serenity had painted it. My hair had been lighter then. "You didn't say anything to Celestial?"

126

He shook his head. "I went to the Sand Bar to summon up my courage, then drove back to her house. Through the kitchen window I saw Celestial and her friends eating dinner with the two hippies from the beach, the Frisbee throwers. Instead of storming in there and beating the crap out of them, I stayed in the car. I felt dirty, as if I were the one who'd done something foul. You were in a high chair facing the window. Celestial handed you a carrot stick or something. You smiled and waved it in the air. And you know what I was thinking?"

He paused for a moment, then continued quietly. "I wished I were back in Vietnam."

He stared at the ceiling of the Whale, then closed his eyes. I tried to imagine how he must have felt, watching Celestial with those jerks. They were probably Serenity's friends. If they hadn't been sitting in our kitchen, would Walter have knocked on the door, entered the house, and swept Celestial into his arms? Would he have plucked me from my high chair, tossed me into the air, paraded me around the house on his shoulders? I sighed. "What did you do then?"

"I drove to the airport and caught the next flight to Detroit."

It was too much to comprehend. I opened my door and stumbled from the car. I needed to move, to get away from this man who'd abandoned a baby — me! — because of some stupid prank. I walked up a narrow path, visible in the starlight, to a knoll overlooking the dark ocean. On a rough rock ledge, I pulled my knees to my chest and willed myself to stop shaking.

I tried to make my mind as empty as the dark expanse of ocean below. The rock beneath my bare toes was hard and cold, textured with lichen. I began to pick bits of the scaly fungus from the rock and rub the fragile pieces between my fingers till they disintegrated. Then I picked off more. I thought about how old the lichen was, hundreds of years, and here I was destroying it. But I couldn't stop. I felt as old as the lichen, felt torn away from my world, my rock, crushed to bits.

A car door opened and closed behind me. Then Walter appeared at my side. He shook off his blazer, draped it around my shoulders, and sat down beside me on the rock. We watched the stars.

"I used to think about your mother when I was out on night patrol. She'd tried to teach me the constellations, but they all looked different there."

I nodded. "She showed me too. She must have told me at least a hundred times about the hunter and the bear. The sisters. Gemini. Pisces. The scorpion. I can remember some of the names, but I can't find them anymore, except for the dippers and Orion's belt." I pointed to the three bright stars in a row. When Walter leaned against me to sight down my arm, I could feel him shiver. "Why did you come back to Arena after all these years?"

"Mostly because of Owen."

Owen, not me. What had I expected — an overwhelming surge of guilt and sudden outpouring of fatherly duty? I thought of the kid in the photograph, my half brother. Besides sharing freckles and the same father, what did he have to do with me? "Were you looking for a replacement for him?"

I felt his body stiffen. "Owen is not replaceable."

"I'm sorry. I didn't mean that. It was a dumb thing to say." I should have bitten off my tongue.

"Forget it," he said. We could have been on opposite sides of the mountain, for all the closeness I felt with him then. "Look, Tee, this may take a while to explain, and I'm freezing my tail off. How about going back to the car?"

I was cold, too. My feet were so numb I could barely feel them. I stood up slowly and hobbled down the trail beside Walter.

"Come on. We'll waste my gas," he said, opening the bashed-in door of the Cadillac for me. It moaned with the movement and hung crookedly from its hinges. My fault that Walter had gone off the road? He swiped the grass from the bottom edge of the door, closed it firmly, then ran around to the other side, hopped in, and started the engine. In a few minutes, heat poured over my feet. They began to itch as the numbness wore off. "Put them up here," he said. "Your feet."

I pushed my feet across the leather seat. He set them

129

on his thighs and began to rub them. Did that mean he still liked me, even after what I'd said about replacing his son?

"Better?"

"Yes. Thank you." I wiggled my toes, then relaxed while Walter dug his knuckles into the soft flesh under my arches. He did seem to know about feet. "You were going to tell me why you came back to Arena last week."

He pulled my big toe till it popped, and gave it a little shake. Then he started on the others. "Let me back up a little," he said, as he kept pulling and popping and shaking.

"When I first told Wendy about you, she asked me how I could be sure you were my child. Maybe my war-warped imagination was playing tricks on me. I didn't even know the age of the baby in the high chair. For all I knew, one of the men I'd seen at the table that night could have been your father, Serenity your mother. And even if you were mine and Celestial's, what could I do — take you away from her? Visit you twice a year? Confuse you with a lifestyle and philosophy she'd rejected? If I made myself known to you, Wendy argued, I'd only upset Celestial and make both your lives more difficult. Even though I had doubts about Celestial's parenting, I was less sure of myself and my own grip on reality. I knew she'd take better care of you than I would then." He pressed my toes gently between his hands.

"Wendy and I promised each other we wouldn't dwell on past mistakes. Abandoning a child wasn't exactly an admirable act, but was it any worse than the horrors I'd seen and committed in Vietnam? I needed to forget the war and everything connected to it. That included Celestial. I know it sounds callous, but that's the way I felt." His forehead was beaded with sweat. He let go of my feet, pulled a handkerchief from his pocket, and wiped his face, wincing as he came to the nasty gash on the side.

"Does your head hurt much?"

"Only when I frown." He stuffed the handkerchief back into his pocket. "Warm enough?" I nodded and tucked my feet beneath me. Walter turned off the motor.

He told me about borrowing money from Wendy's parents to open the shoe store. Told me about Carter and Owen being born, then Melissa. Told me how he'd become a pillar of the community, a Rotary Club member, deacon of his church. He joined the country club, paid taxes, played golf, traded in his car every three years. Sure, he was bored with life, but what could you expect? What could ever compare to the excitement of war, the intensity? He had a brief affair with a customer, confessed to Wendy, and was surprised by her vehement reaction. He apologized, she forgave. They both went on with their contained, predictable lives.

"When Owen drowned, I was thrown completely

off balance. At first I couldn't believe he was dead. I kept walking into his room to ask if he wanted to play catch, to tell him to shovel the walk or clean the basement. I blamed myself for his death. If I'd spent more time with him, taught him how to be more careful, he would still be alive.

"A few weeks after the funeral, I collected every potentially dangerous thing in his room — his chemistry set and his Swiss army knife, his bow and arrows, even his shin guards for soccer. I hauled everything out to the back yard, poured a quart of kerosene over the lot and torched them. Brilliant, huh?" He snickered grimly.

"After the fire, I stopped going into Owen's room. I hurt so much I could hardly stand up. I couldn't eat, couldn't sleep. I spent my days in bed reading spy novels, nights in front of the television watching old movies. Anything to keep my mind occupied. But nothing worked. My God, how I hurt."

He blew his nose again and didn't talk for a few minutes. I felt something very uncomfortable inside me, something small and black and hard. Then I realized it was jealousy. I was jealous of the emotions Owen had kindled in Walter. Jealous of a dead boy.

Walter continued. "All that time Wendy held things together. She kept the store open, got Carter and Melissa off to school, answered sympathy cards. She even raked up the ashes in the back yard after my fire. We barely spoke to one another for a month." He shook his head.

"One day I finally managed to make an appearance at the store. I retreated to the back room between stacks of shoe boxes and stared at inventory lists for a few hours. When I got home, I heard a commotion in the kitchen. I walked in the back door and saw Wendy in the middle of the room throwing groceries. She smashed eggs on the refrigerator, splashed milk on the floor, fired a loaf of bread at the cupboards. When she saw me she threw a head of lettuce in my face. She yelled about how selfish I was, screamed that she hurt and missed Owen just as much as I did, that she was sick and tired of pretending she was strong so I could grovel in my pain. That she had loved him, too, and still did. Then she burst into tears.

"Right then, I felt Owen in that trashed kitchen with us, laughing at us and at the mess we'd made of things. God, I loved that laugh. I loved him. And that love was more intense than anything I'd ever experienced, including my guilt over his accident or the pain following his death. Even more intense than the war." He reached over and put his hand on my shoulder. "Still listening?"

I nodded but kept my mouth shut. I was afraid all the vile blackness might rise from my gut and spill out, revealing me for the ugly, jealous person I was.

"You see, in Vietnam I learned to protect myself

from going crazy by not caring. I didn't form close friendships, so I wouldn't be destroyed when the boys I commanded died. Yes, I felt sorry, but I didn't fall apart. I survived. Later, at home, I blocked out the whole experience. Except for the occasional nightmare, I just didn't think about the war.

"When Wendy and I got married, I kept up the barriers. I liked her a lot but wasn't exactly consumed by passion. And having kids was fine, once they passed the diaper stage and could swing a baseball bat, but nothing to get excited about."

He cracked his knuckles, then sat quietly for a minute or so before continuing. "Somewhere along the line I let my guard down. All of a sudden, standing in a puddle of milk that day in the kitchen, I realized how much I loved my family. I loved my wife and kids. I loved Owen. Loved his freckles and bruises and the cowlick that stood up on his head, loved the fact that he was always busy, always curious, always trying something new. Even though I should have known better, I loved him."

I bit my fist. Why couldn't he love me like that? He was my father too.

"And then it hit me. My love for Owen was still alive. The love I felt was somehow an indestructible entity. If I hadn't loved him, hadn't allowed myself to feel, he would be dead. But because I loved him still, he wasn't really dead and never would be."

Was it true? If someone loved you, would you live forever? I hated questions like that, questions without answers, and had to sit on my hands to keep from flailing them in the air or ripping out my hair in frustration.

"So," Walter went on, "what did all this have to do with the baby in California? Once I realized I'd been fooling myself about Wendy and the kids, it wasn't so hard to examine my feelings about that baby. I was curious and ashamed. I had to find out if the child I'd seen in the backpack was mine, had to face what that meant for me.

"I didn't intend to hurt you when I came to California. I love you very much, Tee, partly because you are my daughter, partly because you've become a very special person. And I don't want any more lies between us. You deserve the truth."

What a screwed-up world. My father had loved my mother but she hadn't loved him. She got pregnant and had me and loved me. He went off to war and killed a bunch of people and watched a lot of people get killed and stopped loving everybody. Then he saw me and didn't love me. Ran away. Got married. Had three kids and didn't love them. Then one of them died and he decided he really did love him, loved them all. Then he came to find me and decided he loved me.

Was this the truth Walter spoke of?

Suddenly I was bawling like a baby, sobbing for all

the years I didn't have a father. Weeping for my mother, who loved me in her own strange way. Crying for Owen, who'd died before his father realized he loved him. I cried for Walter because he'd learned how painful love can be. I cried for myself because I wasn't sure who I loved or why.

I soaked my father's shoulder with tears.

Chapter 11

Dear Tee,

Wendy and the kids met me at the airport last night. We stopped on the way home for dinner. I thought about you while I ate my double bacon burger and fries — not nearly as juicy as the Snack Shack's nor half as tasty as your artichoke frittata.

Melissa didn't stop talking all evening. She lost a tooth and gave herself a haircut while I was in California, looked like an orphaned jack-o'-lantern. Carter was mad at me for missing his triumph with the debating team and didn't speak all evening. Were you ever an angry adolescent?

Wendy is trying to adjust to the idea that a large part of my heart (sorry, don't mean to be so

*sappy) is centered on a person she has never met.
I've tried to reassure her that loving you does not
diminish my love for her and the kids, but she is
only beginning to trust the new me. How could
she know that my love would expand so rapidly?*

*Should I be confiding to you about my wife,
my marriage? Are you ready for this intimacy? I
don't want to put you in an awkward position,
but I do think of you as my friend as well as my
daughter. Perhaps this frankness is one of the few
advantages to emerge from our lack of history together.*

*By the way, do you have any spare snapshots
of yourself? I know Celestial doesn't believe in
taking them, but I would very much like to have
a photograph of you. I miss those freckles of yours.
Maybe Skeg or Turbo has a camera? I'll be happy
to pay for film and developing.*

*This evening we called a family meeting and
told Carter and Melissa about you. Carter's reaction: "Gee, Dad, you really screwed up." Ever
the tactful member of the family, he wanted to
know if you might suffer any long-term psycho-
logical damage because of my blunders. He also
wondered if you would share equally in any inheritance. (Maybe he knows about some secret
Swiss bank account I'm not aware of.) Melissa is
thrilled about having an older sister, especially
one who repairs cars. Keeping her priorities in*

perspective, she wanted to know if you wear glasses and have straight teeth. They were both disappointed in me for running away from you after the war and are trying to deal with this latest confirmation of their father's inadequacy, a quality they discovered long ago.

All three of them are anxious to meet you, although Carter would never admit such a weakness. Will you please reconsider a visit to us this summer? You wouldn't have to fly — there is Amtrak service from Oakland.

I'm enclosing a check for $200, yours to use as you see fit. Count on this amount every month. I have complete faith in your judgment on money matters and on what to do after graduation. I realize you're confused now, but I really believe the answers will come if you relax and stop trying to take care of everyone in your life.

That is friendly, not fatherly, advice. I don't expect you to listen because we share the same gene pool. Do know that I love you and care about what happens to you. Remember you will always be welcome here.

Walter

April 19

Dear Terra,
My heart goes out to you for all the confusion you must be feeling. I just want to tell you how

much your father loves you. Walter is a wonderful man but has his shortcomings, as we all do. If he was wrong to leave you with your mother when you were an infant, then I must share the blame for that decision with him. Maybe we both made a mistake, but we did what we thought was best for you.

You may not realize how worried he is, he jokes around so much. He tells me you understand why he stayed away all these years, but inside he is desperate for your forgiveness. He never did apologize to Owen for holding back, so Owen never had a chance to forgive him. A few words from you would make a big difference to him.

God bless you,
Wendy Spray

Dear Tee,

I am happy to have a girl relative. I have five boy cousins and there are nineteen boys in my class but only seven girls. Mom says you are only my half sister, but I'll take what I can get. I miss Owen a whole lot but don't miss having two brothers poking around in my busyness. I guess I miss you half as much as Owen since you are only half my sister. And besides I have never met you I hope you will come to our house soon. You can sleep in my bed. If you want. I'll sleep on the floor. I

promise not to wake you up. Dad says teenagers
could sleep through anything.

> *Hugs and kisses from*
> *your 1/2 sister Melissa Agnes Spray*

May 2

Dear Tee,

You're very welcome. I'm glad they fit. Let me
know if you need socks or extra laces.

This will be a short note as I have to be at a
Chamber of Commerce dinner in half an hour.
Would you believe that your father is introducing
the keynote speaker, the biggest Pontiac dealer in
Michigan. I will think of the thrill of shark fish-
ing with you in order to stay awake through his
speech.

About school . . . Why are you so worried about
French? I have every confidence in your ability to
pass the course. Please don't quit. You have only
a few weeks left. Finishing now will be much
easier than going back later. Bonne chance!

One other word of advice. (Keep reading.
Please?) Skeg is a fine person, but there are plenty
of other young men who would appreciate your
wonderful qualities as much as he does. Explore
your options and don't let Skeg pressure you into
doing anything you don't really want to do. On

141

the other hand, don't hold back because you fear
involvement. Enough said.

Time to put on a tie and hit the road.

Love,
Walter

May 9

Dear Tee,

Sorry to hear about the new mechanic. No, I
don't think Turbo can be sued for religious dis-
crimination. If the guy actually quit, and it
sounds from your letter that he just walked off
the job in righteous indignation, then the big boss
should be OK. Maybe next time he should inter-
view a few more applicants instead of taking the
first guy who walks in off the street with a
wrench in his hand. I wish I'd been there when
Turbo caught him preaching to the customers.

The vending machines should have arrived by
now. Turbo needs to call the distributor and find
out what the hang-up is. Has he heard anything
from the bank or the S.B.A. yet?

I don't know what to say about Celestial. The
time she channeled for me was interesting, but I
honestly don't know if I was talking to anyone
other than your mother. Everything "Astraeus"
said could have been said by Celestial, including
the Greek references. (I seem to recall her telling

me about a classics course she took at Berkeley.)
Still, the rhythm was off, if you know what I
mean. I pay a lot of attention to the way people
walk. Everybody has a distinct gait, a unique
way of putting one foot in front of the other. I
have an eerie feeling that, if I'd seen Astraeus on
his feet, his walk would have been entirely dif-
ferent from Celestial's. (Am I trying to persuade
myself that he is real?)

As for his more frequent appearances, I don't
think you should worry, at least as far as Celes-
tial is concerned. According to the research I've
done, a vehicle can't be taken over unless he or
she wants to be. Like hypnosis. Or self-hypnosis.
Have you talked to Celestial about this?

In any event, try not to let the channeling upset
you.

Much love,
Walter

Hi Tee!
I didn't go to school today. I have a runny nose.
Mom calls it a spring cold and says I got it
walking home with wet shoes after me and my
friend Jessie caught Polly wogs two days ago.
Mom yelled about the shoes. Dad brought me new
ones from Walkabout. All of the Polly wogs have
tails. Owen used to catch a bunch every year and
keep them in his old goldfish bowl til they tirned

into frogs. Then he brang them back to the pond and let them go I miss him alot.

When are you coming to see us? Do you have Polly wogs in California?

We taped your picture on the refrigerator next to the school lunch menu. Mom cried when it came. She thinks you look like Owen. I don't. I think you look like Judy G. in the Wizard of Oz. What is your favorite movie? I hope you come soon so I can see if you look the same as your picture.

Love,
Melissa Spray

May 18

Dear Tee,

The S.B.A. wouldn't tell me anything about Turbo's application. You are taking a big risk on the loan but, as I said before, the money is yours to spend as you wish.

We're getting ready for a big Memorial Day sidewalk sale — my last chance to get rid of the spring inventory. Maybe I should be clearing out the summer models as well — I'm already up to my eyeballs in next winter's catalogues. When did the retail business start rushing the seasons? I'd like to enjoy the lilacs before I start thinking about raking leaves — Walter's words of wisdom for the week. Hey, do you think that's market-

able? Maybe we should go into fortune cookies —
you do the baking, I'll write the messages.

No, I haven't seen Apocalypse Now. *Or any*
of the other Vietnam movies. Maybe it's time I
did. From the way you describe him, I'd say that
Brando's character is not all that far from real-
ity. If you come for a visit, maybe we can brave a
trip to the theater together or rent a few videos.
Will you hold my hand if I get upset?

Keep me posted on the gas station. Ask Turbo
if he'd like to convert to shoes.

Au revoir,
Walter

Hi Sis! Thank you for the coloring book of reptiles
and amphibians. Next to frogs, I like iguanas
best. Do you have iguanas in California? Are
there any iguanas in the oshun? I have never seen
an oshun, just Lake Michigan. Oh, and I saw
Lake Huron once when I was a baby but I don't
remember it. Dad says it looks almost like the
oshun except the waves are smaller. Carter says
you can swim easier in the oshun because of the
salt. I would like to check if he is right. Maybe
some day I will visit you and we can go swim-
ming. I am a pretty good swimmer, even tho I
can't see too good in the water without my glasses
on. My eye doctor says I can get contact lenses
when I stop growing. But I don't know if you can

ware them swimming. The worst thing about glasses is they are always getting steamed up when I need them most. Also I can't see at night after I take them off. Once when we were camping I wore my glasses to bed in my sleeping bag so I could watch for shooting stars. In the morning when I woke up they were broke. I slept on top of them.

You should be happy you don't have to ware them.

Bye for now,
Melissa

P.S. The Polly wogs have back legs now.

May 19

My father suggested I write to ask your opinion. I would like to take apart and rebuild an engine for my final project for physical science. I have two questions: 1. How long will it take me? In other words, can I do it in three weeks, considering one of the weekends is Memorial Day and I have three consecutive days to work, in addition to afternoons after school. 2. What kind of engine would be best?

I would appreciate an answer as soon as possible, so I can go to the junk yards next week.

Thank you for your assistance,
Carter Spray

Chapter 12

The letters from Michigan piled up in my sock drawer. I read and reread them all at least a dozen times but still wasn't sure what to make of this family of Walter's that apparently was my family, too. I felt as though I'd stripped down an engine, reassembled it, and wound up with a bunch of extra parts. I didn't know where those superfluous parts belonged. The engine worked without them.

I had enough to do at home without worrying about a spare family several thousand miles away. I needed owner's manuals for the two unreliable vehicles in my immediate life — a 1947 mother with electrical malfunctions and a classic friend with a tendency to overheat. I needed trouble-shooting guides and illustrated, step-by-step repair instructions.

At the top of my clipboard was Turbo. Nothing went right for him. The Small Business Administration lost his loan application and made him fill out a pile of forms all over again. A small cash advance he managed to get with a credit card did nothing to appease the landlord. The four hundred dollars I loaned him barely covered the price of candy and soft drinks for the new machines. Then one of the machines broke and had to be replaced.

He hired a full-time mechanic, a former Baptist minister who walked off the job after three days of listening to Turbo's foul mouth.

Curtis, the next guinea pig, was painfully shy. He avoided female customers and only talked to me when we were working on a job together. Even then, he never looked directly at me. His work was steady and meticulous. He really knew Japanese engines, had spent a year in Tokyo studying karate and aikido, Hondas and Subarus.

Despite the extra help and income, Turbo remained depressed and angry. He complained about everything I did and criticized Curtis for hours on end. He fumed about the weather, politics, the decay of Arena Beach, anything that attracted his miserable attention. One day Curtis quietly suggested he try yoga or Zen meditation. Turbo told him to shove the mystical garbage up his nose.

I did my best to ignore these tantrums and kept hoping the SBA would come through before Turbo blew a gasket or threw a rod.

Meanwhile I also fretted over Celestial. She flipped

out more each day, went into trances when there were no clients around, sat transfixed for hours at a time, saying nothing. She lost twenty pounds, became pale and subdued. What on earth, or in whatever unearthly realms she visited, was happening to her? Was Astraeus, like some voracious cancer, increasing his own strength by devouring her?

I missed Walter. He could have teased me about Celestial and convinced me she'd be all right. Although he was doing his best to cheer me up from Michigan, his letters and phone calls didn't have the same force as his presence.

Skeg and I watched a few Vietnam movies on Turbo's VCR. The films made me sick and very, very sad, but they helped me understand my father's experience over there and what he'd faced when he came home. I forgave him for leaving me years ago, but I still ached over his recent departure.

I worked frantically to keep my life — and everybody else's — in running order. I flew over the mountain from school every day and checked in on my mother. Then I dashed down to the station, put in a few hours' work for Turbo and tried vainly to cheer him up. Then I raced home again, fixed dinner, and begged Celestial to eat.

Every night I pumped my brain with French. I had to get my grade up to a C in order to graduate, and I was determined to do it. I conjugated verbs, composed complex sentences, and attempted to fathom the differences between the *passé composé* and the *imparfait*. I went fishing with my father: *J'ai pêché avec mon père*. Owen used to go fishing with his father: *Owen allait à la pêche avec son père. Mon père, aussi*. I recited long lists of vocabulary words out loud, asking Celestial to help me. More often than not, she'd space out in the middle of a lesson and I'd have to finish it myself.

In the midst of all this, Skeg and I managed to squeeze in a few hours here and there to explore our new relationship.

Turbo decided to stay open all three days of Memorial Day weekend to milk the extra tourist business. When I arrived at the station early Saturday morning, he was polishing the pumps and grumbling about the fog. "That pismire of a weatherman promised sunshine. Who the hell's going to come to the beach in this crap?" But by nine o'clock the fog was lifting, the thermometer heading into the seventies — perfect beach and running-out-of-gas weather.

Curtis crept in around ten. "Who the hell said you could take the morning off?" Turbo snapped.

"I don't work Saturdays," Curtis said softly, blushing and tugging on the single gold stud he wore in his ear. "I just stopped by to pick up my paycheck. Do you need some help?"

Turbo scratched out a check, ripping the paper slightly, and shoved it in Curtis's face. "Get out of the way, jackass." He pushed past Curtis into the shop. Curtis left quietly.

Rush and lull, rush and lull. Either there were four cars lined up on each side of the pumps, or no one pulled in for fifteen minutes. When the pumps were clear, I helped Turbo in the shop. When customers fumed impatiently, I dashed outside to wait on them by myself, grateful that Turbo was keeping his black mood indoors. I grabbed burgers to go from the Snack Shack before the afternoon exodus began. Then, as soon as people started leaving the beach, I pumped gas and washed windshields nonstop till closing.

"Come on, genius, I'll treat you to a Coke at the bar," Turbo said. Even the invitation sounded grumpy.

"Thanks, but I told Skeg I'd drop by the Lip on my way home." I ignored his leer. "Would you like to have dinner with us later?" Maybe Celestial could make Turbo smile.

"No, I'll just drown my worries in beer. Besides, I'm not fit to eat with a herd of hogs in heat these days."

I grinned, preferring grossness to grouchiness. "That's okay. I know you've got a few things on your mind." A tiny cut on the back of my hand stung like crazy when I wiped my greasy fingers with a rag soaked in gasoline. I looked at Turbo out of the corner of my eye. "Does your doctor know you're drinking?"

"Piss off." He gave me the finger, then waddled across the street.

Skeg turned the key in the front door of the Lip, hung the CLOSED sign in the window, and pulled me upstairs to his loft. "I thought those grommets would never leave," he said as he peeled off his T-shirt.

I'd watched him wait on three adorable boys who looked at Skeg as if he were some kind of god. They spent half an hour talking surf talk, selecting a wrist guard, a package of Sex Wax, a couple of stickers for their skateboards. Skeg had been sweet with them at first, then less and less patient, especially after I came behind the counter and started to tickle his waist under his shirt.

"You shouldn't rush your customers. Not if you want them to come back," I said. I kicked my shoes in the corner, pulled my shirt off, and unbuttoned my jeans as fast as I could, grateful we didn't have to mess with condoms anymore.

"I never rush anyone," he said, tossing his shorts over his shoulder.

"Of course not." I stared hungrily at his body and pushed my jeans and underpants off together. He tackled me to his mattress, laughing. His hands smelled of coconut oil and wax. My hands smelled of soap and gasoline. His sheets smelled of salt water and sunshine.

We'd come a long way since that first time on the

beach. Skeg had taken an HIV test. I'd been to the gynecologist for an exam and birth control pills. We'd become, well, more efficient, I suppose.

But I often felt, over and above the physical exhilaration and satiation, a shadow of regret. Not for my lost virginity. How could I believe that was a precious commodity after my Harmony House upbringing? I guess I missed my innocence, or maybe my independence.

Afterwards we wrapped up in beach towels and shared a bottle of Gatorade from his refrigerator.

"Tom called this afternoon. He wants me to meet him in Oceanside a few days before the contest next weekend." He took a long swig of Gatorade and handed the bottle to me.

I drank and passed the half-empty bottle back to him. "Can you afford to skip that many days of work?"

"I've already lined up a couple of dudes to keep the store open. Why don't you come with me, babe? Relax, soak up the rays. Watch me shred some killer tubes."

I leaned back against his chest, felt his warm skin against my back. It was tempting. "I can't. Exams start in two weeks."

I got up and began to dress.

"Hey, babe." He grabbed my ankle. "How about moving in with me after you finish school?" Something in me stopped, like a wheel locking suddenly, while Skeg continued to talk. "The view's not great, but the rent is cheap. And you can walk to work from here."

Why couldn't he be satisfied with the way things were? Why did he have to keep asking for more? Just when we'd reached a comfortable relationship, why did he have to go and spoil things? I pulled my shoes from the corner.

"I didn't mean to scare you," he said, running his fingers up and down my freckled arm while I tied my laces. "I love ya, babe."

"I love you, too." And I did. Loved his sweetness and strength, loved his dreamy face and the way he treated his mother and the way his eyes sparkled when he talked about pulling some floaters or catching some major air off the crest. I thought about him surfing next weekend in Oceanside, his body strong and tanned and beautiful, thought about all the surfer groupies who swarmed to the competitions, about all the girls who followed their favorite pros up and down the coast. "But I can't move in with you. I have to stay with Celestial. She needs me. "

Chapter 13

I didn't go to Oceanside with Skeg. Instead I went to classes, worked at the gas station, and studied.

"How about a walk?" I asked Celestial after two and a half hours of French one evening.

She looked up from a shawl she was embroidering and rubbed the small of her back. "That would be lovely." She shook out the shawl and held it up to the light. "What do you think?"

Delicate butterflies flitted across the gauzy lavender fabric. Pretty, but much more fragile than the designs Celestial usually created. "It's nice. Who is it for?"

"No one particular," she said. "The gallery will take it on consignment."

That meant we'd have to scrape up next month's rent somehow. Walter's check would help. Maybe I shouldn't have loaned Turbo the other money, but it was too late to change that now. Oh well, if business kept picking up, Turbo could pay me back soon. We'd pulled in lots of cash over the holiday last weekend. "Come on." I pulled Celestial to her feet. "Let's hike up to the water tank."

The night air was balmy — rare for the northern California coast, even in June. We climbed the narrow, winding streets past the hillside homes, then hiked the dirt fire road to the big wooden tank that held much of Arena's water supply for the dry season just beginning. I thought about the letters from Michigan in my drawer. I never added one to the stockpile without worrying that they'd stop coming, that I would hit my own dry season soon. If I decided not to visit them, would Walter and his family eventually lose interest in me? Not entirely, but I knew they'd back off, that the flood of attention I was getting now would dwindle to a trickle. I was hoarding those letters for the drought that was bound to come.

"What have you heard from Michigan lately?" Celestial asked.

"I hate that."

"Hate what, darling?"

"When you ask me a question about something I'm thinking of at that very moment."

"Why do you hate it so much?"

"No one should be able to read someone else's mind. Thoughts are private." I chewed on my nails.

"Are you so ashamed of them?" She looked sideways at me, half smiling. "If it makes you feel any better, I didn't realize you were thinking about Michigan just now, and I don't usually perceive details, at least not details that you don't want to share. I was thinking about my own father as we were walking, thinking about how he would have marched straight up this hill without pausing or even breathing heavily. And thinking of my father reminded me of yours. That's all."

"Reminded you how?" I had never met Celestial's parents. Her mother died of breast cancer when Celestial was in high school. After her mother's death, Celestial and her father had little to say to each other. She could hardly wait to go away to college, to be free of his macho army mentality. When Celestial appeared on national television during a draft-card-burning demonstration in People's Park, he phoned Celestial's dorm and told her in no uncertain terms that she'd better straighten up and stop betraying her country. Then he demanded a full apology. Celestial tried to talk to him about freedom of speech and constitutional rights, but he hung up on her. She wrote him a long letter explaining how she felt and what she believed. He never answered that letter and, from then on, returned all the letters and Christmas cards and birthday cards she sent him, unopened.

When I was a baby, she hitchhiked to Fort Ord, near Monterey, and found the trailer park where he lived. His new wife answered the door. After Celestial introduced herself and me, the woman asked us to wait outside. Celestial heard her father's voice through the thin metal walls, even saw the curtains stir, but the woman came back to the door alone. "He says he doesn't have a daughter or a granddaughter. I'm sorry," she whispered, dabbing her face with a Kleenex before closing the door.

My grandfather never saw or spoke to Celestial or me again. He died in a small-plane crash when I was three. Later his wife mailed Celestial a photograph she'd found in his desk. The picture shows my mother, about ten, standing with her parents under a palm tree with an army tank in the background. In the photograph only my grandfather is smiling.

"I was thinking about my father's pride and obstinacy, which reminded me of how difficult it must have been for Walter to admit he'd made a mistake. I'm glad he told you the truth. That's a good indication of the kind of person he is and of the respect he has for you." She patted my shoulder. "My father didn't respect me. As far as he was concerned, I'd been manipulated by a group of traitors and was so blind I couldn't see the treachery of their acts."

"But why didn't he change his mind when the war ended and the whole country agreed it was a mistake?"

"The whole country didn't agree. People like my father thought the only mistake was that we lost. He had to think that or give up everything he'd ever believed in and worked for." She sighed. "Anyhow, I'm glad about Walter. He's a nice person, don't you agree?"

I nodded. "Are you sorry he came back?" I asked.

"What ever gave you that idea?"

"You. You've been strange since he left. You know, Mom, weird." I flashed bug-eyes at her.

"You always say that about me."

"This time you've been promoted from space cadet to moonship commander. I figured maybe it had to do with Walter."

"You mean you're thinking I'm in love with him and pining over his absence?" She smiled. "That's a sweet, romantic notion, but it's not true." She sighed again. "Oh, it was wonderful to see him. To see how he's changed. Grown. And I do love him, but not in the way you're imagining. It's just that his visit raised a lot of issues I haven't confronted in a long time."

I moved closer to her and bumped her shoulder with mine. "Like what?"

"Oh, like individual and societal responsibility. Purpose." She stared at the sky. *If there was a black hole up there,* I thought, *she would disappear into it.* "You know, if anything ever happens to me, Walter would take care of you."

"What do you mean?" I was startled and looked sharply at her. Her eyes were beginning to glaze over. I was losing her again. Damn! How could I rescue her from something I couldn't see or touch? How could I save her from her own black hole? "Celestial," I said, nudging her ribs.

"Hm?"

I grabbed for the first thing I saw. "Tell me about the stars."

She gave her head a little shake and smiled at me. "All right." When she tilted her head, her hair cascaded down her back and touched the ground beside me. "Look straight up and a little to the left. The brightest star? That's Arcturus, and the kite-shape above it is Boötes. Now drop your eyes halfway to the ocean, as if you're following the kite's tail. That other bright one, over the Farallones, is Spica. Spica's a part of Virgo. It's actually two stars that we see as one. Now move a little to the left and down just a tad. Can you make out the wide isosceles triangle on its side with its tip pointing toward Spica? That's the constellation Libra, your sign. Do you see it? Do you see the scales?"

They were beginning to come back — the names, the positions of the stars, the constellations. I remembered Celestial climbing up to the roof of the barn at Harmony House with Serenity and Monarch and Rose, remembered how terrified I was as I stood at the base of the ladder and watched her feet disappear over the eaves, how relieved when she climbed down after a few minutes, leaving the others on the roof giggling and smoking pot. Celestial took my hand and walked me to the edge of the garden, lay down on a patch of grass, pulled me to her side, and pointed to the sky. I remembered the smell of lavender and basil and tomatoes and earth, especially earth, solid and reliable under my back, so different from Celestial's soft body beside me. I burrowed into her side and watched the sky until my eyes grew heavy. Then she stood up and pulled me to my feet and led me into the house, up the stairs to my mattress on the floor under the window at the end of the hall. She brushed a kiss on my forehead. Then she floated down the hall and descended the stairs as slowly and silently as Venus setting in the western sky. I repeated the names of the constellations over and over again to myself until I fell asleep.

Now Celestial was hardly breathing beside me. "Where's Pegasus?" I asked, needing to hear her speak again.

"Behind the mountain, near the northern horizon at this time of year. We'll be able to see it again in late July or early August." She stretched her neck and glanced over her shoulder. I followed her gaze past Polaris. "Do you remember the story of Pegasus and Bellerophon?" she asked.

I shook my head no. "Tell me."

As she turned toward the ocean, her mane of hair settled over her shoulders.

"Pegasus was a beautiful winged horse who sprang from the head of Medusa. He could soar through the clouds, was free, unfettered by earthly ties. Once he created a magical spring by kicking the earth with his hooves." I dug my heels into the ground. The new

161

running shoes Walter had sent didn't make much of a dent.

"A young man named Bellerophon decided to tame Pegasus. With a golden bridle given to him by Athena, he captured the horse, mounted, and flew into the sky." Celestial gestured toward the stars. The shawl that fell gracefully from her arm was an outstretched wing, the fringe, tips of feathers stroking the earth.

"Bellerophon and Pegasus had many adventures. Together they destroyed evil monsters and savage armies and saved the lives of many people. But Bellerophon wanted more than the earthly fame he had attained with Pegasus' help. He wanted to become a god. He cajoled the reluctant horse into flying higher and higher toward the slopes of Mount Olympus."

She pulled the shawl around her shoulders. "The gods didn't want a mortal on Mount Olympus. The next time Bellerophon approached the heights on his friend's back, the gods sent a fly to sting Pegasus. Bellerophon was thrown and fell to earth. Some say he died instantly, others that he crawled away, gravely injured, and died later. But Pegasus was rewarded for his bravery and beauty and purity and allowed to visit Mount Olympus whenever he wanted."

I closed my eyes and saw the magnificent horse, wings unfurled. The horse was Celestial, her mane braided with sparkling beads, her eyes gleaming. But Astraeus snuck up on her and captured her and forced her to do his bidding, to fly higher and higher, to ap-

162

proach the gods. I saw Astraeus in Bellerophon's Greek robes, goading Celestial on toward the heights. Then I saw her buck and plunge, saw her toss Astraeus off her back, saw him plummet to earth. I opened my eyes and looked at the stars glittering coldly above the bay. If Astraeus kept driving Celestial away from this world, what would happen to her when he fell?

Chapter 14

Finals. *Finalement.* The end of my high school career, if I could get at least a B– on my French exam. I tried to psych myself up as I showered. *Réussir.* To succeed. *Réussir à un examen.* To pass a test. *Je vais réussir à mon examen français.* I am going to pass my French test. *Avec un* B. *C'est possible?*

Too nervous to eat breakfast, I stopped at the station for a Coke on my way out of town. Curtis stammered a "good luck" and disappeared into the shop. Turbo handed me a small bag of corn chips from the new display. "Just take it step by step," he advised. "Like following a repair manual." Easy for him to say.

The student parking lot was crawling with zombies who'd stayed up half the night cramming pointless facts into their already warped minds. I hurried inside as the warning bell sounded.

"Bonjour, classe," Madame Bonneau, otherwise known as The Mole, said as we filed past her desk and took our seats. Only the A students answered her greeting.

The bell rang. My mouth went dry, my stomach tightened. I knew I shouldn't have eaten those corn chips. I stared at the first page and drew a total blank. I couldn't remember Turbo's advice, couldn't remember anything. I looked around the room. Heads bent over desks. Pencils scribbled furiously. I felt sick.

Madame Bonneau gave me one of her best rodent looks. I cupped my hand over my mouth and tried to concentrate. Take it a step at a time, Turbo had said. I wiped my sweaty palms on my jeans and began to fill in the first blank. *Nom:* Terra Bliss.

Centuries later, I turned to the last page. Extra credit. *Expliquez une différence entre la culture de la France et la culture des États-Unis. Utilisez votre imagination.* I glanced at the clock. Four minutes left. What would Turbo do in this situation? Quickly I scratched a picture of a fat American tourist in Paris, dressed him in a Grateful Dead T-shirt and overalls. The tourist, English-French dictionary in hand, stood in front of a Parisian street vendor and a cart of fruits and vegetables. *Les fruits et les legumes,* I printed quickly. In a balloon coming from the American's mouth I wrote, "Avez-vous les oeufs plantes?" The street vendor, in the bubble over his beret, pictured a large house plant with eggs hanging from its branches like fruit. Beneath the whole cartoon I wrote *L'aubergine*. The eggplant.

The closing bell screamed. I drew one more egg, turned the test over, and heaved a huge sigh that felt more like a death rattle. Madame B. scurried down the aisle, snatched the papers off my desk, and spoke to me in squeaky English. Didn't she think I could understand the French for "See me after school"?

The physics final wasn't exactly a piece of cake, but I worked through it and finished early, grateful that Turbo had explained the Theory of Chaos so many times.

I was feeling better until I walked into Madame Bonneau's classroom. The Mole bared her front teeth at me. "I thought you would like to know about your test results as soon as possible, *Mademoiselle* Bliss. The office notified me that your grade in this class is critical to your meeting the requirements for graduation."

I licked my lips. Why didn't she just tell me?

"Asseyez-vous, s'il vous plait."

When I sat in the chair beside her desk, her garlic breath nearly blew me away. Did The Mole eat escargots for lunch?

"I realize you have found this class to be very difficult, *Mademoiselle. Très difficile.* I have spoken to some of your other teachers, and they assure me you are not lazy. Can you explain why your grades have been so poor here? Is it my method of teaching, perhaps? Some kind of resistance to learning a foreign language? You know, there are many benefits to studying a different language and culture." She squinted at me behind her thick glasses. I shrugged my shoulders.

She opened a file folder. Inside sat my exam with a big red −36 on the first page.

"*Mademoiselle,* you are still having the problems with the irregular verbs, *n'est-ce pas?* I am sorry you did not come to see me after school this semester. I could have given you help with this and with some of the other difficulties you demonstrate *ici.*" She tapped another page of my test with a red pen. "*Et ici.*" She turned to another page, as bloody with corrections as the Battle of Waterloo.

Then she flipped to the last page and pointed to my cartoon. "I must say that your understanding of the French culture is superior to your grasp of the language, and I know you have worked very hard." Her beady eyes glittered and her lip twitched. She raised her hand from the page, revealing the big +20 she had inked under my cartoon. A large red B in a circle stood out at the bottom of the page. "So I have doubled the normal extra credit for your drawing. *Félicitations, Mademoiselle. Vous avez réussi à l'examen. Et le cours.*"

I almost hugged her, garlic breath and all. Instead I managed to blurt out a stupid *merci* as she handed me my test. Mercy was more accurate. I could hardly wait to show my cartoon to Turbo.

*　　*　　*

I breezed up the mountain in the Whale, singing *La Marseillaise* aloud. *"Allons enfants de la patrie,"* I croaked tunelessly. *"Le jour de gloire est arrivé."* The day of glory *had* arrived. I was free. No more school. No more irrelevant classes and boring teachers. No more commuting over the mountain every day. I didn't even care that the road slug in front of me was doing about ten miles an hour and refusing to pull over to let me by. Life was great. From now on, I'd be able to keep a closer watch on Celestial. I could spend more time with Skeg, maybe even get to some of his West Coast competitions. I'd work full time, help Turbo salvage the business, earn a decent salary, and still have plenty of free time. *"Marchons, marchons."* I tapped the horn and laughed out loud.

On the road shoulder ahead I spied a large bird with tropical plumage — Celestial in one of her brighter costumes. She waved her wings and stepped aside as I pulled over and stopped. "I passed!"

She smiled into the open window. "That's wonderful, darling. Congratulations. How does it feel? Aren't you proud of yourself? Do you have room for an old lady?"

She looked anything but old in a pair of fluorescent pink balloon pants, an orange and purple quilted vest over a filmy yellow shirt. And a very white, very new pair of Walter's walking shoes. But she was so thin and pale I wanted to stuff her with cheesecake.

"What are you doing?" I asked.

168

"I was out walking and thought I might catch you if I waited here." Her eyes swept the horizon where a thin line of fog separated the ocean from the sky. She turned toward me and spoke quietly. "Tee, I have some bad news. Turbo died this morning."

My elbow cracked into the steering wheel as I spun toward her. I stared at her face and knew it was true, knew I had expected something like this for a long time. Slowly I reached for the key and turned the engine off. "Another heart attack?"

She pressed her lips into a thin line between her teeth and took my hand and squeezed it gently. "No. Apparently he drove his motorcycle off a cliff on the coast highway. Intentionally."

Her bright colors hurt my eyes. I turned away. "He looked almost happy when I saw him this morning." One step at a time, he'd said when I fussed about my French exam. Had he thought about committing suicide one step at a time? Or had he just straddled his Harley, raced down the coast, and flown into the air without thinking it through? He hadn't even yelled at me in the morning. I should have known something was up, should have stayed with him instead of dashing over the mountain to take a stupid test. I could have distracted him, could have talked to him about the Theory of Chaos, and reminded him that all random motion eventually resolves into patterns, that there is meaning in chaos. Why did he do it?

Celestial pulled something from her pocket. "He

169

left this on his desk in an envelope addressed to you. I'm afraid the sheriff's department kept the original. Mike Kelly let me make a copy."

I unfolded the sheet of paper. The handwriting was surprisingly delicate for such a big man. "Dear Genius," I read out loud. "The hardest thing about this is picturing your disapproval. I've named your father executor of my estate. After all the bills are paid, the rest is yours. Maybe he can salvage a set of sockets for you. Now get the hell out of Arena and do something with your life."

He was still trying to tell me what to do, still giving me orders. Who did he think he was?

"Don't be too hard on him," Celestial said. "Curtis told me about a notice that came from the Environmental Protection Agency a few weeks ago. They gave Turbo ninety days to put in new gasoline storage tanks. They said the old ones leak."

He told Curtis but not me. Curtis, who had worked with him for only a month, who wasn't even his friend. I bit my lower lip. "I'm sure he didn't want you to worry. Especially with your exams coming up."

"The EPA. Great. Some protection." Celestial patted my hand. A red-tailed hawk circled overhead, gaining height with each revolution around an invisible column of air. "Curtis was probably too cowardly to stop him."

"It's not Curtis's fault, sweetie. Turbo sent him to the Snack Shack for coffee. When he got back five minutes later, Turbo was gone. He phoned Turbo's house but didn't get any answer, then checked the bar. He even called me. Finally, when Turbo still didn't show up, Curtis opened the note and dialed the sheriff's office. An hour later, Mike Kelly found where Turbo's bike had gone off the road. Gus and Larry climbed down to get him but had to call in a helicopter. He was too heavy to carry up the cliff."

I could picture Gus and Larry rappelling down the rocks to the ocean's edge, could see them strapping Turbo's huge bulk to a stretcher, then attempting to haul it back up to the road. I could almost hear Turbo laughing at them and telling dirty jokes while they struggled. "He would have liked causing all that trouble."

"Yes, I believe he would," Celestial said softly. I slid across the seat toward her and put my head on her shoulder. We sat there for a long time, watching the fog move all the way into the bay, across the beach, then up the mountain until it surrounded us.

Chapter 15

A few days later I met Mike Kelly, the deputy sheriff who'd found Turbo's body, at the station. The sheriff's department had already changed the locks, so Mike let me into the office and watched while I removed my personal things. In an old Pennzoil carton I packed my coveralls, a pair of work gloves, the Tigers cap Walter had left behind, a single flip-flop, and a coffee mug Monarch had made at Harmony House. I found the old *Popular Mechanics* I'd been saving with an article about reupholstering car seats and asked Mike if I could take the '64 Buick repair manual. He said he couldn't imagine anyone else wanting it. I picked up an ashtray from Turbo's desk and rubbed through the ashes to the letters painted on the glass: AVALON HOTEL, CATALINA ISLAND.

"Finished?" Mike asked awkwardly.

"Yeah."

I tucked the ashtray into my box, then loaded the box in the trunk of the Whale while Mike locked up. Then I drifted across the street to the Lip, feeling totally at sea.

"Hi, babe," Skeg said gently. "How ya doin'?"

"Okay, I guess." I told him about the ashtray. "Did Turbo ever say anything to you about going to Catalina?"

"Don't think so." He put his arm around my shoulder and led me to the back door. "Check out my new board." A surfboard with a rough sketch of a curvaceous mermaid leaned against the outside wall.

"It's nice."

"It's supposed to be you." I'm not sure which one of us was more embarrassed. We both squirmed.

"Thanks."

He picked up a pencil and added a few more scales to the mermaid's tail. "Did you find out about the funeral?"

"There isn't going to be one. Mike said Turbo's mother is having him cremated." My voice cracked a little.

Skeg put the pencil down and held me. I closed my eyes against the tears.

We stood like that for a few minutes. Then I wiped my face with the back of my hand. "Can I borrow your raft?"

* * *

I lugged Skeg's rubber raft across the street and hit it with a blast of air at the station. Then I popped it on my head and carried it to the beach.

By the time I plowed through the breakers, I was soaked to my waist. I adjusted the plastic oars and began to row toward the reef, concentrating on my strokes. I enjoyed the strain on my arms and my back, the routine physical motion that took my mind off everything else, for a few minutes at least.

Several hundred yards from shore, I pulled in the oars and drifted into a thin patch of fog. A crappy day for business, Turbo would have said, or something more gross. I leaned back in the raft and watched the fog swirl past in gauzy shreds. Avalon was supposed to be the place where King Arthur went when he died. Was Turbo there now? Had he found a bit of paradise?

I drifted past a few pelicans, then more. In a little while I was in the middle of a huge flock of them, bobbing up and down on the swells. They squawked at each other and rustled their wings in occasional territorial dispute.

The fog grew thicker and thicker till I could barely see the beach. My future was equally obscure. Now that the station was closed, I had no job, no income. How were Celestial and I going to pay the rent, buy groceries? Walter's monthly contribution would help, but it wouldn't be enough, not unless Celestial channeled for more paying clients or sold more needlework than she had recently. She'd been working on a new sewing project, a special order, she'd told me, so at least we wouldn't starve this month. But what about next month and the ones after that? Arena wasn't exactly bursting with career opportunities. Maybe I could wash dishes at the Snack Shack or make beds at the Dunes.

Walter said it might take months to sort out Turbo's estate. He had no idea whether anything would be left for me. When I'd called to tell him about Turbo, he offered to fly out for a few days, but I told him to save the plane fare.

"You realize there's nothing you could have done to stop him, don't you, Tee?" Walter had asked over the phone.

"Celestial said the same thing."

"How is she?"

"About the same, I think." By which I meant terrible. She had lost more weight. Dark circles hung below her blue eyes. But Walter obviously didn't want to hear about her.

"Have you made any decisions yet about visiting us this summer? Never mind. Forget I asked. This isn't a good time for you to be making any decisions. Why don't you just relax for a few weeks? Take up French cooking. Go fishing."

That reminded me of the graduation gift he'd sent. "Thanks for the tackle."

Now I dropped my hand over the side of the raft and dragged my fingers through the cold water, thinking. I should have brought my new pole along. At least I might have caught dinner.

I must have dozed off. The next thing I knew, the raft was riding the breakers toward the beach, backwards, tossing and bucking. A huge wave crashed over the bow. The stern rose like a breaching whale, then slammed down on the water and buckled. I plummeted to the ocean bottom, not sure which way was up, then clawed my way blindly to the surface, spitting sand and salt water, gasping for breath, cursing my own stupidity.

"I made some tea," Celestial said as I came out of the shower.

"Good. Let me get dressed first." I pulled on some old sweats and a thick pair of wool socks and joined her at the table by the window. Outside, the fog was so thick that the next-door neighbor's house looked like something out of Sherlock Holmes.

"I hope it's sunny for your graduation tomorrow. I'd much rather sit outside than in that stuffy gymnasium."

"I don't think I'm going." Celestial cocked her head at me. "I can pick up my diploma in the office later. Or ask them to mail it to me." Turbo would have poked merciless fun at my graduation, would have razzed me about my cap and gown, would probably have given me the finger or held up a placard saying CONGRATULATIONS, GENIUS. I would have participated in the ceremony if he'd been here, just to see what he'd do. Now the idea of celebrating seemed pointless. "Commencement," they called it. What was I commencing?

"Well, it's up to you, darling. Here," she said, sliding a cardboard box across the table. "You can use this for a bathrobe."

I opened the lid of Celestial's box and pulled out a long black robe. Traditionally the seniors at Sequoia High decorated their graduation gowns. Some painted political statements or glued on meaningful symbols: tennis rackets, volleyballs, drafting tools, beer cans. One guy last year was asked to turn his inside out for the ceremony because he'd drawn a sexy nude on the back of his robe with her arms reaching around to his crotch area.

"I hope it's not too silly," Celestial said, her voice tentative, hopeful.

I lifted the robe — the "special order" she'd been working on lately — from the box and held it up to the milky light from the window. Near the hem were embroidered waves, row after row of them, with a few surfers riding the curls to the beach where miniature shore birds with glass bead eyes poked their beaks into the sand. The mountain rose steeply from a cluster of Hansel-and-Gretel beach cottages. On its slopes Celestial had stitched green grass, clusters of poppies and iris, deer browsing in a clump of lupine, a stream bubbling under a wooden footbridge. The mountain road, a twisting length of lavender grosgrain ribbon, curved toward the neck of the gown. On the left shoulder a smiling orange sun cast sequinned rays. On the other shoulder a silver Pegasus flew through appliquéd clouds toward a thin yellow moon.

I knew Celestial meant well, but the mythical paradise she'd created had nothing to do with reality. In the real world of Arena Beach, fog blanketed the bay and the sun rarely shone. On the mountain, wildflowers and grass withered in the drought. Deer went hungry. People died in automobile accidents.

I examined the robe again and decided the stitching was lumpy, the figures all out of proportion, the beading sloppy. What had happened to Celestial's fine hand and eye? What was happening to her mind?

I looked across the table at her. She stared out the window into the fog.

"Celestial?"

No answer. She was off again, off in another world that was about as real as the one on my graduation gown, a world made of dreams, not weeds and thistles and dirt, an imaginary paradise where sunbeams cascaded like waterfalls, where fish frolicked and birds soared and deer slept undisturbed in lush meadows, a world where horses sprouted wings and flew, where even the crookedest mountain road presented no danger.

How could I bring her back to reality? I gathered the robe into a pillow on the table and laid my head on it, observing her. Her eyes were open, but she wasn't seeing me or anything I saw. Her lips were parted slightly, as if waiting for a kiss from the handsome prince. While I watched, her lips began to move.

"Terra, how may I help you?"

Oh, God, it was him.

"Terra, you wished to speak with me?"

"No," was all I managed to whisper hoarsely.

"You may not be fully aware of your request, but you called me here to ask for my help. Is this not correct?"

No, this was *not* correct. The last thing in the world I wanted was a conversation with this creep. Oh, God, I was going to puke.

"You'll feel better if you relax and breathe deeply."

How did he know how I felt? I buried my face in the robe, drew bunches of the silky fabric to my ears. Blackness all around. If I moved my head slowly back and forth, I could block out everything else and hear only the hissing of the surf. After a long time, I raised my head and wiped my mouth with a corner of silk.

Celestial's head rested against the windowpane. Her face was almost as white as the fog on the other side of the glass. She rolled her eyeballs toward me and smiled a thin smile, then spoke in that ghostly voice that was nothing like her own. "Are you feeling more comfortable now?"

I nodded slowly, determined not to let him get to me. I was in control here.

"Terra, don't be frightened. Celestial has been experiencing some significant disturbances lately, but she will rise above the turmoil and return to you with her heart and all her lesser senses intact. Now," he said, heaving a great sigh, "you have been thinking of consulting me. I have also wanted to converse with you for some time but could not do so until you were ready."

"I *never* wanted to talk to you," I said, pleased by the forceful sound of my voice.

Silence.

I fiddled with the silver Pegasus on the robe, traced the outline of wings, head, hooves. I could feel two intense eyes burning into my skull. Without looking up I mumbled, "Why was my friend Turbo so unhappy?"

"Ah, yes. Turbo. The physicist. Francis was a man of great knowledge but little wisdom. In his university studies he learned about the interconnectedness of all matter and energy, but in his life he saw only fragmentation. Apparently he could not reconcile the two points of view."

A lot of fancy words and no real answer. "Lots of people have lives that don't make sense, but they don't all drive off cliffs."

"Ah, but many people are not aware, as Turbo was, of the possibilities available to them. Your friend understood the implications of $E = mc^2$. He had studied the Reality of Potentials theory and recognized the importance of the observer in any understanding of reality. Unfortunately he experienced great difficulty

180

moving from observer to participant in his own life." Celestial stroked her chin thoughtfully, a gesture totally foreign to her. "Perhaps he despaired of ever participating, of ever actualizing, in this life."

Despite my best intentions, I found myself listening. I even began to catch the drift of what Astraeus was saying. Turbo had spent a lot of time standing around and griping, telling people what to do, blaming everyone else for what went wrong in his life.

What about me, I wondered. *Am I an observer rather than a participant, too?*

"You move from observing to participating each time you drive over your mountain, Terra," he said without being asked. "But your potential reality extends far beyond Arena Beach."

I looked at him sharply. "Are you saying I should leave Arena? Please don't give me any garbage about relativity and potential. Just tell me what I should do."

"I realize, Terra, that you are very concerned with answers, with solutions. I can tell you that you will not find the answers you seek in your father or your mother. Nor will you find them in an encyclopedia or at the end of a fishing pole or even in a bed. The answers to the greatest mysteries already exist within you."

"Bull. If the answers are in me, why don't I know them? Why can't I see them? And what good are you? I thought spirits, or whatever you call yourselves, were supposed to give advice, answers. Aren't you like a guardian angel or something? A spirit guide? Well then, *guide* me.''

He didn't say anything, just stared out the window into the fog, or made Celestial stare.

I gritted my teeth, determined to force at least one answer from him. ''Why did Turbo deliberately desert me? He knew I planned to stay here and work for him and take care of Celestial.'' I hated myself for being such a whiner. Still, I was very, very angry with Turbo. He knew I depended on him. Dying didn't solve his problems, didn't turn him into a success or a gentle person, didn't do anything productive for anyone else either, especially me. What good would inheriting his tools do? I needed him to teach me, to ground me in a world of wrenches and gaskets and valves and pistons, a world that could be diagnosed and fixed. Suicide was no solution. Only an end.

''But he did teach you. Didn't he leave you a note? Perhaps he wanted to make things easier for you by narrowing your options.''

''No!'' I pounded the table with my fist. Celestial appeared unmoved. ''If that's true, then that means I caused his death. He died because of me.''

''No, he died because of himself. You know that.''

Yes, I knew, but it didn't make me feel any better.

Suddenly, more than anything, I wanted to be with Skeg. He really loved me and cherished me, wanted to take care of me. He wasn't crazy. He wasn't depressed.

His dreams weren't of another world, only of another wave in this world. I could get into that.

"Could you though?" Astraeus asked. "Could you be happy following someone else's dreams?"

"But what if being with Skeg *is* my dream?"

He didn't answer.

Dreams. Was that what life was all about? Was Celestial's channeling a kind of dream? Had Walter dreamed Owen's presence and been healed within the dream?

Perhaps the real reason Turbo died was that he failed to dream.

What, then, were my dreams? What did I really desire? I wanted my mother to be conscious enough to love me and to care about what happened to me. I also wanted her to be able to take care of herself, not because I resented having to do things for her, but because she was an adult and should be independent, responsible. I wanted her to be happy, too. I wanted my father to be around when I needed a sensible opinion or a shoulder to cry on, but, even more, I wanted him to have the strength and integrity to stay with his other family. I wanted him to forgive himself. I wanted Skeg to stay sweet and kind and free-spirited.

"You know, Terra, you are extremely perspicacious and generous when it comes to deciding what's best for everybody else, but what about you? What do you want for yourself?"

183

"I don't know," I whispered. "Can't you give me any hints?"

Celestial stroked her chin and stared out the window. In the distance a foghorn moaned mournfully: no–o–o–o–o.

After a few minutes of silence, Celestial yawned, then blinked her eyes rapidly and stretched her arms above her head. "Do you think the robe is too silly, darling?" she asked in her own voice, her gaze falling on the graduation gown I still held in my arms. Tranquil ocean, sunny beach, lush mountain, benign mountain road.

I shook out the robe and pulled it on over my sweats. "No, it's not silly," I lied.

Chapter 16

Walter hired a lawyer to straighten out Turbo's estate. The lawyer consigned all Turbo's worldly goods — tools, spare parts, cartons of oil and other vital fluids, repair manuals, leftover paint, furniture, T-shirts, and overalls — to an auctioneer.

Skeg came to the auction with me. A middle-aged man in a tweed sport coat and another guy in greasy coveralls with "Buster" embroidered on the oval patch on his pocket waged a bidding war over a set of Snap-On wrenches. I ran queasily to the ladies room. While I was gone, Skeg bought me a mismatched set of sockets that needed derusting.

We stayed for the whole sordid affair. The biggest surprise of the day was Turbo's ashtray collection. In addition to the dozen at the station, hundreds more had turned up at Turbo's apartment. The entire collection sold to an antique dealer for twenty-seven hundred fifty dollars. I thought about how Turbo would have laughed at that dealer's foolishness every time I dropped my loose change into the Avalon Hotel ashtray on my dresser.

In July Turbo's former landlord, the actual owner of the property, sold the gas station. When the new owners began to remodel, they discovered rot throughout the entire structure. Heavy equipment rolled into town and demolished the cracked tile roof and freshly painted stucco walls. So much for Pegasus and his high hopes, I thought, as I watched a bucket-loader pack the debris into large trucks with deep beds. The old storage tanks were dug up and replaced by new, environmentally safer ones. Twelve brand-new stainless steel and enameled pumps were installed before the townspeople realized what was happening. Then there was a lot of yelling and screaming in the county planning offices, and the whole project was shut down for being inconsistent with the local coastal plan. The new pumps were ripped out, a chain-link fence erected around the site.

Meanwhile the residents met at the community center and argued. Who were these new owners? Had they bothered to ask anyone who lived here whether Arena needed a modern self-serve station with an eighteen-foot canopy, much less a mini-mart? On the other hand, if the property were zoned for a gas station, who had any right to tell the new owners how

186

many pumps they could install? Where would the tourists, not to mention the locals, buy their gasoline if the station didn't reopen? Where could the fire trucks, the ambulance, fill up? How was anybody going to get a car repaired?

As the political issues became more tangled, empty soda cans and broken beer bottles accumulated on the lot. Bits of paper and plastic blew into the fence and stuck there. The stubs for the new pumps protruded from the dirt and rusted in the salt air.

I felt sick every time I drove by on my way to work. Bill Stuart had hired me to do the baking at the Snack Shack. I started at three-thirty each morning so that fresh bread and pastries would be ready for the breakfast crowd. In the predawn darkness, the desecrated gas station lot looked like a nuclear bomb site. Even Turbo, who didn't give a hoot about appearances, would have been horrified by the destruction.

Skeg's ratings on the U.S. Tour had been rising steadily all season. Although I missed him when he was out of town competing, I also enjoyed the simplicity of my life on those days. I usually finished work at the Snack Shack by ten in the morning and, instead of watching Skeg wait on customers or shape or glass a new board, I puttered around the house, tried out new recipes, and talked to Celestial. I patched the rust spots on the Whale and repainted her. Then, with Celestial's help, I reupholstered the seats, front and back.

Since Turbo's death, Skeg hadn't mentioned my moving in with him. He seemed reconciled to the status quo as far as I was concerned.

Surfing was something else.

"If I can place in the top five this year, I might get an offer from one of the big companies — OP or Ray-Ban."

"What kind of offer?" I asked as I watched the muscles of his back ripple over his latest creation — a longboard for a local middle-aged surfer.

"A place on the World Tour." He blew an errant forelock of straw hair from his eyes, avoiding my look of incredulity.

"Are you that good?"

He shrugged his shoulders modestly. "Tom says I'm not half as aggro as I should be." He stood back to check the smoothness of the wax layer he'd just applied to the deck of the board. "Ya know what's strange? I don't really care about beating everybody else. I just want to be the best I can be, surf the best waves. That's what the World Tour would mean — Hawaii, Fiji, Australia. Think about it . . ." His eyes traveled to the far corners of the globe.

I expected him to suggest I travel with him, but he didn't. "What about the glory? All those beach chicks drooling all over you," I said, unable to keep the jealous edge from my voice. "You must get turned on by that part of winning."

He blushed. "I already have a beach chick." His waxy fingers stuck to my skin when he kissed me.

In August, the U.S. Pro Surfing Association scheduled two consecutive weekend competitions in southern California. Skeg decided to drive down the coast and stay for both of them. I agreed to meet him in Malibu for the last day of the second contest. Then we could drive back to Arena together in his VW.

I arranged for a few days off at the Snack Shack and made a big lasagna that would last Celestial a week if necessary. Then I packed a small duffel bag with a few clothes and more than a little ambivalence. I knew about all the wild parties that seemed naturally to accompany surfing competitions, about all the gorgeous, bikini-clad beauties that hung around the surfers. Not exactly my style, I thought as I shoved a black maillot into my bag. But Skeg had asked me to this event at least a dozen times, had said I'd bring him luck.

I wasn't sure I wanted to bring him luck. If he surfed well at Malibu, he might be offered that position on the World Tour. That would mean — well, I didn't even want to think about the consequences of his success. Maybe I could put a voodoo curse on him, make him fall off his board, wipe out at a critical moment.

Nervous and excited at the same time, I hopped a Greyhound to Los Angeles. I twisted and turned uncomfortably on the narrow seat of the bus as it barreled south through the central valley all night. Eventually I dozed. I dreamed about water, about swimming in the ocean. I was a baby dolphin. A big dolphin swam protectively beside me. She was my mother. I nuzzled her belly, turned upside down, and nursed as we swam. She made happy dolphin squeaks. Then she wasn't my mother anymore. The big dolphin was Skeg teaching me to play. We leaped over waves together. We soared and dove and sent sparkling fountains into the sunny sky. Suddenly, the Skeg dolphin beside me turned into an enormous shark, sleek and sinister, but I was still a young dolphin. I thrashed my tail and flailed the water convulsively. The evil shark fell back in the murky water, then torpedoed up behind me and opened its huge jaws and —

"Ouch!" The bus, making a wide turn on a city street, lurched across a curb. My head hit the window glass. I blinked my eyes in the morning light while the driver announced we had reached L.A. I spotted Skeg's VW parked out front as we pulled into the terminal.

Malibu, home of movie moguls and screen stars. The houses weren't nearly as impressive as I'd imagined, but the beach crowds were overwhelming. Hundreds, maybe even thousands of people waited for the day's competition to begin. Skeg deposited me under a big beach umbrella with Shelley, the wife of his fellow surfer Tom, and their baby girl.

Shelley talked all morning about the party she and Tom had attended the previous night with the baby. Tom had gotten totally ripped and Skeg had helped her carry him back to their motel. "Skeg's such a doll. Do you think you two will get married soon? He talks about you all the time."

"I don't think either of us is ready to settle down," I said, pulling the elastic on my bathing suit down over my buns.

"That's what I said until I got pregnant with Malia." The baby was fussing. Shelley dragged her back onto the blanket, brushed the sand from her sticky face, and lifted her to her chest. Under the over-sized men's shirt she wore, Shelley slipped off the top of her bikini and began to breastfeed Malia. I looked away. "Tom thinks it's epic, traveling all over with a baby, but he doesn't have to feed her." Shelley had only a few years on me, but she seemed a great deal older.

"Look. There goes Skeg," she said without much enthusiasm.

Skeg was first in the line-up. He found a slot and was instantly on his feet when another surfer dropped in on him and cut him off just as he began to carve. A lot of people in the bleachers booed.

"Interference," Shelley said. "The judges never see

it." She switched Malia to the other breast. "I guess Skeg told you he and Tom are tied for second place? God, what I could do with three thousand bucks!"

No, Skeg hadn't told me, but I nodded, not wanting to reveal my ignorance. I watched Skeg paddle back out and take his place in the line-up for another shot. He'd have to do some pretty fancy maneuvering this time to make up for that last ride.

When the baby finished nursing, Shelley placed her in a frayed wicker basket and readjusted her bikini top. "Tom's up next. Would you mind keeping an eye on Malia while I go watch?"

I told her to take her time. I wasn't about to leave the shade of the umbrella in the midday sun. I just hoped Malia didn't wake up crying. I wasn't any more equipped than Tom to feed her.

I didn't see the accident. There were too many people standing in the way and I couldn't leave Malia to investigate. But I heard the crowd gasp in unison, then heard the announcement on the loudspeaker requesting people to move back and clear a space. Someone had been injured. *Not Skeg,* I whispered, *please not Skeg.*

I watched Malia open and close her fingers as she slept, oblivious to the crowd and the noise. She didn't even wake up when an ambulance siren screamed away.

At last Skeg appeared with a dark scowl on his face,

leading Shelley toward the umbrella. Tears raced down Shelley's face, smearing mascara on her cheeks.

I jumped up and grabbed Skeg's arm. "What happened?"

"Some Barney slammed into Tom and sliced his knee." He snatched the umbrella from the sand and collapsed it angrily. "I almost punched him out." Skeg nearly hit someone? I couldn't believe it. "Come on, babe, I told Shelley we'd take her to the hospital."

Shelley stood there in a daze while I began stuffing suntan lotion and diapers and sand-covered plastic toys into a large brown paper bag. Skeg jammed the blanket under his arm without even shaking it out.

"What about the rest of the contest?" I asked him softly so Shelley wouldn't hear. "You'll miss your next heat if you leave now. I can drive Shelley if you give me directions."

"I don't care about the rest of the competition," he said darkly. "Come on, Shell, let's go."

Tom's knee took twenty-six stitches. We sat with Shelley and the baby in the emergency waiting room, then drove all three of them back to their motel before returning to the beach to get the car they'd left behind.

Skeg was silent for most of the drive through the bumper-to-bumper traffic. When we reached the beach, the contest had ended, the crowds disappeared. Skeg learned the day's results from a couple of guys who were packing up the portable bleachers. Then he herded me down to the water and strolled pensively through the foamy shallows.

"Are you sorry you didn't stay today?" I asked him, wondering how much effect today's default would have on his ratings.

His eyes were on the waves. "No. Ya know, babe, sometimes I think I'm just not cut out to be a professional surfer. Tom's right. I'm not aggro enough. And I don't want to be. I don't want to hurt anyone." His eyes swept the horizon. He continued thoughtfully. "For the past few weeks, I've been thinking about quitting the circuit. That's the real reason I wanted you here this weekend. I had a feeling this might be my last competition. I wanted you to see it."

"What about the World Tour?" I asked, scarcely daring to hope that he'd given up the idea of leaving Arena to travel.

When he looked at me, I could see the answer in his eyes, see how hard it was for him to tell me. His answer didn't surprise me.

"I'm still going to Hawaii. I just don't think I'm gonna compete anymore."

I swallowed hard. "What will you do in Hawaii?"

"A dude I know from the circuit owns one of the best board shops in the islands. He's got more work than he can handle so he offered me a job. If things work out, we'll be partners in a year."

"That's great," I said, and almost meant it. "Where's the shop?"

"On the north shore of Oahu. Haleiwa."

"You'll get to surf the big waves."

He nodded. "Off-the-Wall. Pipeline. Waimea." He pronounced the places as if they were holy. "I won't ask you to come with me," he said, "because I know what your answer would be." He swirled the water with a bare toe. "I wish I could tell you what it's like, babe. Surfing. Making love with you is close sometimes. But it's different when I'm out there. I can't explain."

He stared at the horizon. I felt the sandy ocean bottom shift under my bare feet. "Try. Please."

He wrapped his arms around my shoulders and pulled my back to his chest so that I faced out to sea, too. "Look at it. It's like, like Mother Nature, or God, or whatever you want to call it. It's not good or bad. It just *is*."

The sun had already dropped toward the islands. I stared at a tiny cloud reflecting its orange glow. "Go on," I whispered.

"When I'm out there on my board, I'm alone with it, with Nature. Even if there's a dozen other dudes in the line-up, I'm still alone. I watch the waves, check out the sets, wait for an opening. Then I paddle like mad, get into position. I punch the edge, drop down the face, and, if I do everything just right and the wave is just right, if the balance between us is right, I fly. If I'm lucky, maybe I even do a full-on tube ride. It's like, like I'm in a different world. A different time. I'm part of some awesome power. I'm not controlling it, it's not controlling me . . ." His voice faded.

I couldn't compete with that. Couldn't and shouldn't even try. But I was glad he'd found it for himself. Glad, and more than a tiny bit envious. "Thanks."

"For what?" he asked.

"For telling me."

He turned me around and hugged me and hugged me and hugged me. "Thanks," he whispered.

"For what?"

"For listening."

"You're welcome."

We wandered out of the water and drifted up the beach toward the parking lot. There was one more thing I had to know before we left.

"Can I ask you a personal question?"

"Sure."

"Aren't you ever afraid out there, scared of getting hurt, or maimed, or even killed? I saw the look on Tom's face today after the doctor told him he might not surf again. He was *scared*. And I read in one of your magazines about those two guys who drowned last winter in Hawaii." A chill ran up my spine. "Is it worth it — the risk?"

"Risk is part of it. Why I like it. Why I do it." His

eyes began to gleam. "It's like this, babe. You're in some slop, or you get caught in a rip, or you go for the wrong wave or take off at the wrong time. Ya know you're gonna wipe out, ya know that wave's gonna unload right on top of you and pound you into the bottom, hold you down and not let you up till you run out of air. Ya know you're dead. But you say what the hell and you go for it. And sometimes you do wipe out. But other times, other times . . ."

His eyes swept the incoming set. "You're deep in the trough. You lean back on your heels and keep real low, then you bury your rail and drive back up the face. You carve that baby up, stitch that lip for thirty, maybe forty feet, then drop back into the curl. That wave is hangin' over your head, your eyes are poppin' out of their sockets, and you're goin' faster than you've ever gone and you feel a rush like you've never felt before. But it's because you've been so scared that you get the rush. If you didn't have the fear, you wouldn't have the rush. The best surfing's not about competing, about beating everybody else. It's about beating your fear."

I'd never heard such a speech from Skeg. I was in total and complete shock. Abruptly he stopped walking and stared at me.

"Ya know, babe, that's a problem with you. When you're scared of something, like being up high or something like that, you say you can't help it. You get dizzy or you throw up. You say it just happens, that it's a phobia or something, that you can't control it.'' He took my hand and pulled me across the beach. "Come on.''

I dragged my heels in the soft cool sand as he hauled me toward the lifeguard tower a short distance away. "Don't," I said, but he kept pulling me.

He dropped my hand at the foot of the tower and scrambled to the platform at the top of the wooden rungs.

"Come on, Tee, if you can rebuild an engine, you can climb a ladder. It's only a few feet. I'm right here. You can do it. I know you can."

I looked up at him. He was so beautiful, so talented, so strong. And he really did love me. Even though I'd been afraid to move in with him, too scared to make that kind of heavy-duty commitment, he still loved me.

Tentatively I put a foot on the bottom rung of the ladder, then drew the other foot up beside it. I moved my hands up a notch and gritted my teeth. One foot again, then the other. Then the hands. My head rose above the base of the platform. I stared at the sand on Skeg's bare toes. He squatted down and gently wiped the sweat from my upper lip with his finger.

"You're doin' great, babe. Keep it up." He held out a hand.

I swallowed hard and ignored his hand. I could do this myself. I grasped the side rails extending above the platform and stepped up one more rung. Now I was looking at the golden hairs on Skeg's kneecaps. One more rung and I was face to face with his crotch. Another, his bronzed chest. One more, just one more and . . .

"I knew you could do it," he said in my ear as he squeezed nearly all the air from my lungs.

I smiled as wide as the horizon.

Chapter 17

September brought dwindling days of sunshine to Arena, a new manager to the Lip, and postcards to my box at the post office.

Hey Babe. Check out the cool dude on this card. That could be me catching some air in Waimea. I'm practicing every day to be ready for the big kahunas this winter. Miss you, babe. Nobody makes muffins like you. Love, Skeg

Hi Babe! How ya doin'? Business is great. I met Kelly Slater last week. He tried out one of my boards and might ask me to custom shape one for him. I'm glad I'm not surfing against him. Hi to Celestial. Later, Skeg

Hey Tee, what's happening? Finally found a place to live in the hills above Pipeline. I can see the swells coming in from Alaska and pick mangoes from a tree outside the door. Stay cool, S.

Each card seemed to be a little less personal than the one before. What had I expected — long-distance devotion?

I diverted most of my energy into my work. At the Snack Shack, I baked currant scones and five-seed whole wheat bread, cinnamon rolls and blueberry bran muffins, banana sour-cream coffee cake and apricot squares. Old and new customers alike praised my creations. Bill called me *La Pâtissière* — the baker — and gave me a raise.

Every day I brought a tempting selection of pastries home to my mother. I made her yogurt shakes and grilled cheese sandwiches and vegetable casseroles with lots of tofu added for protein. In ever-increasing quantities, she ate them all. By Labor Day, her clothes came close to fitting instead of hanging off her like rags from a scarecrow, and her complexion regained most of its rosy color.

She began sewing again, but not like before. She whipped up new curtains for Bill's restaurant and embroidered the edges with seashells and sand dollars. At once she received orders from half a dozen cafe patrons who wanted identical curtains and matching pillows for their beach cottages. The projects weren't exactly great art, but at least they kept her fingers and mind occupied.

Astraeus had not made an appearance since the foggy afternoon he spoke to me in June. When her former channeling clients phoned, Celestial apologized and explained that she was not doing that kind of work anymore. Walter said I told you so and shipped us each a new pair of shoes for fall.

Melissa wrote to me often. Sometimes she sent newspaper clippings with her letters — car ads from the Detroit papers, a story about cohoe salmon returning to the Great Lakes, a feature on a local German beer festival with recipes for sauerkraut, potato pancakes, and apple strudel.

Occasionally Wendy or Carter answered the phone when I called my father. Talking to either of them was awkward. I always felt very relieved when Walter took over the phone and the conversation. He made me laugh every time, even the day Skeg left for the islands and I burned two batches of bread at the Snack Shack.

"Tee, do you think I could learn to drive?" Celestial asked one morning when I came in from work. My clothes and hair smelled of yeast and flour, my fingertips looked like yellow raisins from scrubbing bread pans for an hour. I bit off a ragged hangnail.

"Sure, but you don't really need to. Is there something you want? I'll drive you over the mountain after I shower."

"Well, I am out of black thread," she said, poking through her sewing chest, "but you don't have to make a special trip for that." She pushed a pretty ceramic thimble onto her middle finger and looked up at me. "I just thought it would be a good idea for me to be able to drive myself. Will you teach me?"

Her eyes were as blue as the tiny windmill on the thimble. What if she got her license and then spaced out while she was driving over the mountain? What if she ran into a deer or went off the road or hit somebody else? She'd never forgive herself if she hurt anyone. But if she went to one of those driving schools and took lessons from someone who didn't know the mountain road, her chances of getting in a wreck would multiply.

"Okay," I agreed reluctantly. "When do you want to start?"

"This afternoon?"

I drove the Whale around the lagoon, past the spot where Walter and I had caught the shark, then headed across the mesa to the north. When the paved road ended, I pulled over and gave Celestial the wheel. She stalled the car, then flooded the engine, so we had to sit and wait for the carb to clear before trying again. This time I was more precise with my instructions, and she was able to get the engine restarted. Slowly she bumped along the unpaved, little-traveled road, gripping the wheel with her two dainty hands at ten and two o'clock. When another car came toward us, she drove into a shallow, weedy ditch. She managed to get the Whale back on the road herself, and after that she did all right. Except for almost hitting a telephone pole on the right when I told her to stay on her side of the road. Except for nearly ripping off my muffler in a deep pothole. And except for running into a bush in the parking lot at the end of the road when she stepped on the accelerator instead of the brake.

I suggested we take a break before heading back. We climbed down the narrow trail to an isolated stretch of rocks and sand where Skeg and I had made love behind a wall of driftwood the day before he left. "Skeg used to surf here," I told her.

She gave my hand a squeeze. "You must miss him very much."

"You know, it's funny. I don't miss him as much as I thought I would," I said, only realizing it was true as I spoke the words.

By the middle of October, the Whale had a collection of fresh scratches in her new paint job, I had learned the true meaning of patience, and Celestial had mastered the necessary skills to take her driving test. We made an appointment for the afternoon of the seven-

teenth, my birthday, then made reservations for a celebration dinner at a French restaurant in Sausalito
where we had a special, two-for-one certificate.

The Department of Motor Vehicles office was
crowded. While Celestial waited in line, I retreated to a
plastic chair against the wall and picked up a *N.Y.
Times* crossword puzzle someone had left behind.
Thirty across: STEW IN PARIS. *Ratatouille* or *bourguignon?*

Across the room, Celestial frowned over the written
test. I wondered if her chances of passing the road test
would be better if she'd worn something more conservative than her orange and purple vest, yellow blouse,
purple hiking boots, and flowered skirt. Maybe she'd
luck out and get an inspector who liked purple.
Thirty-two down was a ten-letter word for lucky, beginning with *f.* All I could think of was *flamboyant.*

"Don't you think that twenty-five miles an hour is
too fast in a school zone?" she said half an hour later,
standing beside me, wide-eyed. "You never know
when a child might run into the street."

"You passed?"

She nodded. "We're supposed to meet an inspector
on the north side of the building," she told me, then
chewed on her lower lip. She wouldn't win any awards
for confidence, but she was still beautiful.

On our way to the car, I gave her a few last-minute
tips. "When you change lanes on the freeway, first

check your rearview, then the side mirror, then look over your shoulder. And remember to use the turn signal."

She smiled. "Yes, mother."

I drove around the building and sat with her until the inspector, a large woman with a double chin and enormous biceps, marched out. The woman glowered at the Whale, pored over my registration, checked my headlights, tail and brake lights, horn, and turn signals, then ordered me to wait while Celestial took her road test.

"Remember — front, side, shoulder," I whispered as I got out of the car. Celestial gave me a blank look as she slid across the seat. "When you change lanes. The mirrors."

"Oh. Yes." She shoved the gearshift into drive.

As I walked away, I heard the inspector bark, "I'll tell you when you can go."

Temporary license in hand and a big smile on her face, Celestial drove us to the nearby shopping mall. Our dinner reservations were still hours away and we were both famished. At a frozen yogurt shop, I ordered a medium peach with boysenberries. Celestial chose French vanilla with carob chips. We carried our treats outside to a tiny metal table under an umbrella in the sun.

"I was so nervous," Celestial said, giggling. "That woman. It was her voice — like a drill sergeant's. Like my father's! When she told me to back up, I thought she said pack up and I thought she meant to pack up all my hopes of —" She stopped talking, cocked her head, and stared past me. Oh, no, I couldn't stand it if she started spacing out again. But she looked at me and said, "Did you feel that?"

"What?"

"Nothing, I guess. I thought I felt the table shake. It must have been a big truck going by." She smiled and shrugged, then toasted me with a paper cup of water. "Well, darling, happy birthday. I can't believe you're eighteen. Just think, you'll be voting in November." She sighed. "When I was your age, I left home and never went back."

"Well, you don't have to worry about me leaving."

She lifted a plastic spoon of yogurt to her lips, then returned it to her dish without tasting any. Then she put her palms on the table, looked at me, and calmly announced that she had joined the Peace Corps and was going to Africa.

"You're *what*?"

"Tee, don't look at me that way. Please?" Her eyes were dark blue and treacherous. "Tee, I'm not looking forward to leaving you, but I'm growing old and rotting away in Arena Beach. I've got to get out and do something productive with my life."

She might as well have punched me in the gut, my stomach twisted so hard. I could barely breathe. So this was why she wanted a driver's license. She'd tricked me into teaching her to drive so she could drive right out of my life!

"What about your channeling? Why can't you do that again?" I couldn't believe I was actually encouraging her to channel. "Or volunteer somewhere. Deliver meals to AIDS patients. Donate blood. Read to old people in a nursing home."

"Tee —"

"Why do you have to go all the way to Africa?"

"Because that's where I've been assigned."

How long had she been plotting this defection? "It won't work," I said firmly.

"What do you mean?"

"You'll never get there. As soon as the Peace Corps people find out about you, they'll fire you. You'll be lucky if they don't have you committed."

"I know you don't mean that, Tee." She sighed again. "I hoped you'd understand."

"Understand what? That you're crazy or that you're abandoning me?"

"Tee, if I try to explain, will you listen?"

Seething, I mashed the berries into my yogurt.

"Tee, when my mother died I blamed my father and his whole macho army trip for her death and decided to have nothing more to do with him or with anything remotely connected to destruction. I was a woman, a creator. I was going to honor my mother's memory by mothering the world."

"Huh." I stirred the berry pulp and yogurt round and round in my dish.

"So I ran off to Berkeley," she continued, "took in every stray cat on Telegraph Avenue, signed up for every feminist cause on campus. I made pretty baubles for women's adornment, moved into a women's commune, even had a baby.

"And none of it, with the exception of giving birth to you, made me feel any better about my mother. Or myself." She leaned back in her chair and stared at me, almost as if she were seeing someone she didn't recognize. "You know, in a way, I've always felt more like a sister to you than a mother."

My mouth was so dry I could barely talk. "You've never been a mother to me," I whispered.

She shook her head slowly, then closed her eyes. A few tears rolled down her cheeks. After a while, she wiped her face with a paper napkin and looked at me again. "I'm sorry, Tee. I did the best I could."

I bit the inside of my cheek, damned if I'd let her see how much she was hurting me.

"When Astraeus began to appear," she began after a long silence, "he was very understanding, never judgmental. He allowed me to get away from myself from time to time. And he even managed to counsel a few troubled people through me. For a time that was enough.

"Then Walter came. It seemed to me that he'd accomplished more with his shoe store than I had with all my art and my channeling. He was such a good father. In comparison, I was total failure. I was truly ashamed, but instead of doing something about it, I started to retreat more and more into that other dimension."

This was news? She'd retreated so far, she'd almost vanished. I pushed my yogurt dish to the center of the table and covered it with my napkin.

"When Turbo died," Celestial continued, "I realized how much my life resembled his. He buried himself in his auto mechanics the same way I buried myself in my needlework. He repaired cars, I made costumes. And we both lost sight of the fact that these were services done for people, for human beings. You know, Turbo's death wasn't so very different from my channeling. We were both trying to escape our inadequacies, our failures."

I looked at her then and, for the first time, noticed all the lines beside her eyes, the deep creases beside her lips. I looked away quickly.

"After Turbo's death, I told Astraeus I needed some time to myself. I wanted to see what I could discover without his assistance. I hiked all over the mountain in a kind of daze, meditating. *What can I do?* I asked myself over and over. *Why am I here? What is my purpose?* Do you think Turbo ever asked himself those questions?"

"How should I know?" I didn't want to think

about Turbo or about any of this purpose garbage. I wished Celestial would just shut up.

But she didn't.

"Eventually I began to see the colors of the trees and the flowers more vividly, to feel more rooted." I could almost picture her sitting beneath a tree, her hair twisting in and out of the bark, her legs disappearing into the ground with the tree's roots, a kind of wood spirit. When I looked at her, she was just flesh and blood, human. A middle-aged woman with a few gray hairs above her ears.

"One day while I was meditating on Mesa Rock, I suddenly thought about the Peace Corps. I nearly joined in the sixties, but Rose and Monarch talked me out of it. I went home and sent for some literature, filled out an application, and mailed it in, not knowing what I'd do if they accepted me.

"Tee, I heard from Washington yesterday. A group that's already in training just lost one of its volunteers. They want me to take a crash language course and fill the vacancy. We're going to help the women in a village in northern Tanzania set up a crafts cooperative and a daycare center." Her eyes were beginning to glow. "Oh, Tee, I'm so excited. I've finally found something useful that I can do with my own skills and energy. You know, I'm the same age now that my mother was when she died. I don't want to waste any more time."

"What about me?" I screamed across the table. An

211

old couple walking by stared at me. "What about using your skills and energy to be my mother for once in your life?"

She looked at me calmly, as if I hadn't yelled a word. "Tee, you've always been a strong person." Then she had the nerve to smile. "You'll be fine."

There was nothing to say. She'd already made up her mind.

"Tee?"

I glared at her.

"Tee, I love you."

Chapter 18

I left her sitting there, her hair shining in the sunlight that slanted under the big umbrella. If she was responsible and clear-headed enough to go to Tanzania, then she could certainly find her way back to Arena Beach without me. She could hitchhike or call a taxi. She could even levitate over the mountain, for all I cared.

I drove the Whale out of the big parking lot at the mall and headed north on the freeway. I had no goal, no plan, not even a direction in mind. I only knew I didn't want to go home, couldn't bear the thought of being with Celestial or returning to Arena.

I took the next exit off the freeway, so angry I couldn't see straight. How could Celestial desert me? What was it about me that made the people I loved leave? First my father, then Turbo, then Skeg. And now, finally, my own mother. Abandoned, deserted, betrayed by all of them, I felt such hatred heating up inside of me I thought I'd boil over.

Before I knew it, I was being funneled right onto the Richmond Bridge. I'd never been exactly fond of bridges, but this time my old acrophobia symptoms threatened to overwhelm me. *So much for Skeg's lifeguard tower cure,* I thought bitterly. And where was Skeg when I needed him? Probably on the beach at Waimea with some big-breasted, suntanned babe.

There was no exit off the bridge and no way to turn around. In fact, the opposing traffic was on the deck above me, making a horrible racket over my head. I had to go on. Up and up I drove, gripping the steering wheel and gritting my teeth. Beneath the bridge, an ugly, rusted tanker churned through the water. I crept across the span in the middle lane while cars whizzed by at dizzying speeds.

At last, the Whale nosed gradually downward, toward shore and safety. When I finally reached solid ground, I pulled into the breakdown lane and stopped. I wiped my sweaty hands on my jeans, blew my nose, and breathed shakily in and out.

Lights flashed in my rearview mirror. Then a uniformed highway patrolman appeared by my car door. "Everything all right, miss?"

If you only knew, I thought. "Yes, officer. Something blew into my eye back on the bridge." I dabbed my face with a soggy Kleenex. "But it's gone now."

"Sure? I can take a look if you want." He leaned forward solicitously.

"I'm sure. Thanks anyway."

He hesitated for a moment, then said, "Drive carefully."

I drove mechanically, blindly, into unfamiliar territory. Thick rush-hour traffic clogged the freeway. After miles of exhaust fumes and short-tempered commuters, I threaded my way toward an exit ramp and finally managed to escape that thoroughly miserable thoroughfare.

I was lost. I drove past ugly warehouses, iron-barred liquor stores, decrepit houses with trash-filled yards. If I didn't get out of this neighborhood soon, I might not make it to my nineteenth birthday. "Happy birthday to you," I began to sing off-key, then stopped when I saw three or four tough-looking guys in black leather eyeballing me outside a tattoo parlor.

"You idiot," I whispered to myself, then rolled up my window and locked the Whale's doors despite the late afternoon heat. If I were raped or murdered, Celestial would probably call it Karma. "You've always been a strong person," she'd said. What did she know?

Beneath a maze of high-speed roads, I finally spotted a freeway sign. I made a sharp left turn and headed for the entrance ramp.

* * *

215

As I merged with the traffic on the lower deck of the two-tiered freeway, my heart began to pound. Another elevated, closed-in space. Great. Then, mimicking my thudding heart, the Whale started to bump, then buck. All I needed now was a flat tire. Before I could even think about where to pull over, the entire roadway, the whole freeway, began to roll and heave and buckle. An ominous rumble rapidly crescendoed into a monstrous roar. Giant slabs of concrete fell in front of me, beside me.

The world exploded in a great flash of light. Then everything went black.

I woke up in semidarkness, choking on the thick, dust-filled air. Each coughing spasm triggered a sharp pain through my body. I touched my face gingerly, felt warm patches of sticky liquid here and there. Blood? I picked a small sliver of glass from my lip. In the dim light I could barely see my fingertips. I closed my eyes against the nightmare, but when I opened them again, the horror was still there.

Beneath my cheek I recognized the new upholstery fabric Celestial and I had installed in the Whale, the knob on the glove box before my nose. The interior of the Whale's roof was only a few inches above my head. I twisted myself around and in the distance spied a window of daylight.

The Whale's side door had sprung halfway open. Slowly I squeezed and wriggled my bruised body past the door hinge, past the buckled front tire, over a pile of concrete rubble, under a cluster of torn and mangled cables. Inches stretched into feet, feet into yards.

Not until I reached the edge of what used to be the freeway could I even begin to stand up. Then, in a half crouch, I looked over the sheared-off edge, down thirty feet to the inner-city street below. Some people were standing down there, pointing up at me and moving their mouths. I couldn't hear them, or anything else. Stunned and bewildered, I lay down beside a broken guardrail, curled into a fetal position, my head to my knees, and willed the nightmare to pass.

All at once my hearing returned. Shouts and sirens, screams and horns ripped through the thick air.

"Hey!" one of the people below shouted. "You up there. Are you all right?"

I peeked over the edge again, then quickly jerked my head back to my knees. Cold sweat erupted all over my body, and I began to shiver.

"Stay where you are. We'll get a ladder."

Just then the entire roadway moaned mightily as thousands of tons of unstable concrete and steel shifted beneath, behind, and above me. *Jump,* I thought. *Better to risk splitting open on impact than to be crushed to death.* But I cowered there, paralyzed, too terrified to move an inch.

That's when I heard it — a cry, too high and pitiful to belong to an adult, too agonizingly self-aware to be

217

a dog whimpering. Moving nothing but my eyes, I strained to see through the rubble. The grotesque shapes sandwiched between the upper and lower decks of the freeway looked like junkyard wrecks compressed to a third their original height. Surely no one could be alive in any of them.

But I heard it again, the voice crying piteously, "Mama, Mama," over and over.

I clamped my wrists over my ears, closed my eyes, and saw Owen falling through the river ice, going down into the cold, black water, disappearing. "Mama, Mama."

As I cowered blindly there, my heart's hammering gradually eased and I became aware of a sharp pain in my stomach. I reached into the pocket of my jeans and pulled out the fossilized sand dollar from Skeg. A good luck charm? I rubbed it lightly against my cheek, then opened my eyes. The sun was still shining through the thick, dusty air.

Very carefully I lifted my head over the edge of the pavement beside the twisted guardrail. Far below, more people milled about and pointed up at me. "Help's coming, girl. Hang on," a tall black woman called.

Suddenly an explosion rocked the cement graveyard. I smelled gas fumes and saw black smoke pouring from wreckage a hundred yards away. I bit my lip and tasted blood. "Somebody's alive in there," I called shakily, indicating the dark pit behind me. "I'm going to look."

Before anyone could talk me out of it, I tucked the sand dollar back into my pocket and forced myself back into the hellhole. The crying seemed to be coming from the other side of the Whale. I wriggled my way over and around the rubble, back to my car, my eyes slowly adjusting to the tomblike darkness. I couldn't get around the Whale, so I crawled back in and across the front seat. The door on the driver's side was jammed. I squeezed through the shattered window, scarcely registering when a dagger of broken glass sliced my shoulder.

Out at last, I crept toward the Whale's rear fender and the remains of a small, red car. The door facing me had been sliced off. Inside, crushed under the steering wheel and a gigantic cement slab, was a woman. Even in the marginal light, I could tell she was dead. And in what was left of the mangled rear seat lay a small boy, his lower body trapped between the front and back seats. One of his legs twisted grotesquely out of sight under the front seat where his mother's body was pinned. I reached in the car and touched his hair.

With a shudder, the boy stopped crying and screwed his head around. He stared blankly at me for a moment, then began to wail once more.

He wouldn't stop crying, no matter what I said. I

promised him I'd be back. Then I crawled through the Whale again and groped my way toward daylight. It took forever, like in a bad dream when you need to run but your feet are planted in cement. Finally I leaned a fraction over the edge of the deck and told the growing crowd below about the boy.

Then I retraced my convoluted path.

I gagged on the sickly sweet smell of blood and the stench of excrement, but I refused to throw up. I patted the boy's head and told him he was going to be all right. Then, grasping at the first thing that came to mind to distract us both, I told him the Pegasus myth. Then one of Walter's war stories. Then I rattled on about Skeg and the way he surfed. I didn't stop talking until a team of firemen and a doctor arrived. By that time the boy was unconscious.

I backed out of the way so they could reach him, but I refused to be taken to a hospital until it was over. The doctor had to cut through the body of the boy's mother with a chain saw, then amputate the boy's crushed leg below the knee to free him. Finally firemen lowered him on a stretcher to a waiting ambulance.

When I woke up the next morning in the hospital, Walter was sitting in a chair beside my bed. He took my hand and pressed it gently.

"You really should come to Michigan. We don't have earthquakes there."

"No," I said groggily, "just blizzards and tornadoes."

He smiled. "How do you feel?"

"How do I look?"

"Not too bad, considering you have a concussion, two broken ribs, and seven stitches in your arm."

"I do?" Gingerly I touched my bandaged shoulder. I vaguely remembered Celestial's driving test, eating frozen yogurt, and arguing with her. But I couldn't recall anything of the hours that followed, didn't know why I was in the hospital. "An earthquake. Is that what happened?"

Walter nodded and patted my hand. He told me how he'd been watching the World Series warm-up on television when a big quake shook Candlestick Park. He and Wendy and Carter and Melissa fretted as the early disaster reports came over the screen. He tried to call Arena, but the circuits were busy. When he finally got through to Celestial, she asked him to fly out right away.

"She knew you were in trouble, Tee."

"How?"

He shook his head. "She just knew."

I couldn't think about that right then, couldn't think at all. I closed my eyes.

When I woke the next time, both Walter and Celestial were there. I was happy to see her, relieved to know that she was safe and not angry with me.

221

My doctor said amnesia was the mind's way of protecting itself from shock and pain. I can see why, now that I've remembered nearly all the horrifying details of that evening. And I'm glad that Julio, the little boy I found in the wreckage, has forgotten almost everything. I hope his father waits a long time to tell him exactly how he was rescued.

Chapter 19

The next day Walter drove me home in a plush rental Lincoln. When we started across the bridge, I took a deep breath and opened my eyes wide. Higher and higher we rode, toward the summit of the span. To the north I could see dozens of sailboats winging across the Bay. To the south sat a big uninhabited island, its steep, red cliffs overhung with green vegetation prominent against the sparkling turquoise water. In the distance ahead rose the familiar silhouette of the mountain, hazy purple in the golden autumn light. As we descended toward the western shore of the Bay, I didn't feel at all queasy.

I lowered the window of the Lincoln and raised my face to the sun. My hair pirouetted in the breeze. Each freckle on my arms tingled.

In the back seat Celestial hummed softly. I turned around and smiled at her, thinking about what she'd told me in the hospital. After I left her at the shopping center, she had bumped into a neighbor who gave her a ride back to Arena Beach. At home she fussed uneasily about, washed a few dishes, straightened out the pillows on the couch, picked up a piece of embroidery, and put it down again, unable to concentrate. When the quake hit, she felt the whole house lurch, saw the big front window quiver, and watched the hanging lamp above the table swing back and forth. A single book tumbled from the shelves beside the window.

"I didn't know where you were, Tee," she'd told me, sitting beside my hospital bed wet-eyed, "but I knew you were in trouble. I tried to focus, tried to picture you, but all I saw was that book falling off the shelf. Then I heard a voice crying, 'Mama, Mama.' Even though it wasn't your voice, I knew it had something to do with you. I was so scared, Tee. You'd driven off in one of your rages. I prayed for that anger to become strength."

Mao was sitting on the porch, looking almost as scraggly as the potted geranium beside him. I scooped him up and buried my face in his fur. When the phone rang inside, I ran to get it.

"Hi, babe. How ya doin'?"

"Hi," I said, very, very happy to be home, to be talking to Skeg, to have Mao purring in my lap. "Celestial said you called yesterday. How's the Pipeline?"

"About half as awesome as you."

224

We talked for nearly an hour about the quake and Julio, Celestial's mysterious clairvoyance, the surfing in Hawaii. Then we seemed to run out of things to say.

"So, ya seein' anyone new?" he asked with feigned nonchalance, the way people do when they want you to ask them the same thing.

"No, not really. What about you?"

"Well, yeah, as a matter of fact I am. Her name is Susan. She teaches kindergarten and makes bamboo flutes for the tourists. She's showin' me how to wind-surf. She, uh, she's movin' in with me next week."

I watched an incoming wave crest and break from left to right. A handful of surfers rode it effortlessly toward the beach. Skeg had always wanted more than either Arena Beach or I had been able to give. "That's great," I said with only a slight catch in my throat. "I'm happy for you."

"Thanks," he said. "Well, keep in touch."

"I will." I stroked Mao's back over and over and watched the waves roll onto the beach until Walter and Celestial came in from their walk.

Walter drove me around the county, tracking down used car ads from the newspaper. This time, thanks to Turbo's expert tutoring, I knew exactly what to check, how to tell if an odometer had been turned back, whether a major accident had knocked any critical parts permanently out of alignment.

I settled on a '65 Plymouth Valiant with one of

those indestructible slant-six engines. Although the tires were bald and the body needed some work, the car had gone only 110 thousand miles and ran smooth as melted chocolate. I bought new tires, changed her plugs and oil, put in a new air filter, and named her the Great White Shark.

A few days after my father went back to Michigan, I woke up to discover poor old Mao curled stiffly against my knees. Since the earthquake, he'd been acting strangely paranoid, always looking over his shoulder, jerking awake at the slightest movement in the house, eating furtively and not very much. When I dug a hole for him under the lemon tree in the garden, I unearthed the time capsule I'd buried there years ago. The tea cannister had rusted through. The photograph of my grandfather had faded beyond recognition. My diary was blotched with mildew. The letter Walter had written to Celestial before he went to Vietnam fell apart in my hands. I threw away these relics from my past but put the crystal earring back in the ground with Mao — a plaything to accompany him to Avalon. I covered him with earth, then marked his grave with a rock from the beach.

I still didn't know what I was going to do. I could stay at the Snack Shack and continue to work for Bill. Or I could look for a job over the mountain that would pay more. I was a good auto mechanic, and there were certainly plenty of people out there who needed one. But I wasn't very enthusiastic about that option. Repairing the Shark had reminded me too much of Turbo. I was still too saddened by his suicide to think about him on a daily basis.

I knew I wanted to do something special, something less mechanical than fixing cars. Something more human. Since the earthquake, that seemed very important.

The first rains came before the end of October. When my alarm went off at three one morning, I heard the faint whisper of water on the roof, smelled the fresh air. I left the Shark in the driveway and walked to work on the shiny, slick pavement, fingering the packet of California poppy seeds in my jacket pocket. The rain had already begun to soak into the dirt of the abandoned gas station lot. I squeezed through an opening in the fence and scattered the seeds all around.

The kitchen of the Snack Shack felt cozy in the drizzle. I hung my jacket behind the door, switched on the lights, and turned on the big oven, then gathered milk, flour, eggs, and yeast contentedly. I scalded a big pot of milk on the range, then dissolved half a cup of yeast in some warm water with a little sugar to nurture the process. Next I poured a twenty-pound sack of flour, a cup of oil, a dozen eggs, a handful of salt, and enough warm milk to hold it all together, into the giant mixer bowl. Last came the foamy yeast. While the big machine with the kneading attachment mixed and pulled and stretched, I whistled an off-key tune and marveled at the dough's satiny flexibility. Then I coaxed the elastic pudding onto the counter, kneaded and massaged it into a smooth pillow, and oiled the surface (like spreading suntan lotion on Skeg's shoulders, I thought dreamily). I covered the glistening dough with a big damp towel, then started feeding bran muffin ingredients into the mixer bowl.

Bill came in a few hours later, as I was lifting a large apple strudel from the oven.

"Morning, Tee." He peered over my shoulder and shook his head, smiling at the golden pastry leaves on top of the strudel. "You looking for a raise?"

I settled the strudel onto a cooling rack and checked the waiting pans of bread dough. They'd nearly doubled in bulk and were ready to bake. "I thought I'd do peanut butter cookies today. And maybe some biscotti?"

"Hold it," Bill said, turning my face toward the ceiling fixture. "You'll get flour in your eyes," he said as he brushed my cheek with a calloused hand. "There."

"Thanks."

Bill tied an apron around his ample waist and began hauling boiled potatoes from the refrigerator. "Julie wants your blueberry muffin recipe. That is, if you'll consider sharing your trade secrets with a friend."

"Well, I might, if the price is right," I joked, easing the bread pans into the oven.

"Did I ever tell you," Bill asked, bent over the cutting board, chopping potatoes for hash browns, "about the class I took with Alice Waters? You remind me a lot of her."

Alice Waters owned one of the most famous restaurants on the West Coast. I reminded Bill of her? Pleased, I smiled and began to gather more ingredients.

The inspiration occurred as I was shaping the peanut butter cookies. I guided large spoonfuls of dough onto a greased cookie sheet and flattened the mounds into circles with the bottom of a large drinking glass. This revelation didn't hit like a crashing wave or a striking shark, certainly not like an earthquake. One moment I was pressing patterns into the cookie rounds with a fork, wondering what I was going to do with the next chapter of my life. Then, very quietly and surely, like bread dough expanding in a bowl, the answer rose within me and I knew.

Celestial and I spent a week or so sorting through our accumulated possessions. We bundled magazines, boxed books, helped each other decide which clothes to pack in our respective trunks.

"I want you to guard this for me until I get back," Celestial said, handing me her antique sewing chest.

"You don't get to keep it permanently, though, not while I'm still alive and stitching." I wasn't sure if it was the allusion to the possibility of her dying or the idea of her entrusting the precious chest to my care that sent shivers up my spine. I promised to take good care of it.

We held a yard sale, displaying remnants of our past lives around the garden — a set of dishes thrown by Monarch, a rug woven by Rose, a pot I'd scorched making my first batch of fudge, our old ice chest and picnic basket. Most of the furniture remained in the house for Curtis and his friend Donald, who were taking over our lease. I was glad someone I knew would be living in the cottage, appreciating its idiosyncrasies and keeping an eye on Mao's resting place. As neighbors and strangers poked through piles of bed linens and old clothes, I smiled and chatted and made change. All in all, letting go of the past was easier than I'd thought it would be.

Thanksgiving approached. Since the Snack Shack was closed for the holiday, Bill and I decided to prepare a traditional family dinner there. Bill roasted a turkey stuffed with cornbread, walnuts, and mandarin oranges. Bill's wife, Julie, nursed their new baby and made a mushroom and onion soufflé for Celestial. I baked fresh dill rolls and three desserts — cranberry apple pie, pecan fudge torte, and caramel pumpkin cheesecake. Curtis and Donald did the mashed pota-

toes and salad. And Celestial created a stunning cen-
terpiece from seaweed and shells and driftwood. While
she decorated the table, she sang a Thanksgiving
hymn:

*Now thank we all our God, with heart and hand
and voices,*
*Who wondrous things hath done, in whom his
world rejoices,*
*Who from our mothers' arms hath blessed us on our
way,*
With countless gifts of love . . .

When my eyes cleared, I could see her smiling at me
across the table.

On the first day of December, I drove Celestial to the
airport in the Shark. She sailed through the departure
gate in a fuchsia blouse, yellow parachute pants, purple ballet slippers, and a multicolored Guatemalan
poncho. Over her shoulder she carried a canvas bag
that I'd crammed with vitamins. Halfway down the
boarding ramp, she turned around and called, "I'll see
the Southern Cross!" Then she blew me a last kiss.

After I got back from the airport, I called Skeg and
told him my plans. He sounded genuinely happy for
me and asked me to keep him posted, to let him know
how I was doing. I promised I would if I had the time.

Early the next morning I stuffed my own suitcase

with clothes, including the graduation gown that had indeed become a bathrobe, and filled several boxes with tapes, tools, and fishing gear. I packed Turbo's Avalon ashtray in layers of newspaper and secured it between my Walkman and a spare fan belt. I wrapped the exquisite fossilized sand dollar from Skeg in a scrap of silk and tucked it carefully into Celestial's sewing chest. Then I loaded the boxes into the trunk of the Shark with a set of snow chains and a new spare tire.

Packing finished, I wandered through the empty house and stared out the window toward the beach, thinking about meeting my new family. I was a lot less nervous since Wendy had confessed her own jitters to me over the phone. "I don't know how to be the mother of a young woman," she'd said awkwardly.

"That's okay," I told her. "I already have a mother. But I could use a new friend."

I leaned my head against the window and reviewed the Christmas gifts I'd chosen for each of them. For Wendy I'd wrapped the lavender butterfly shawl that Celestial finished just before the quake. Carter's present was unwrappable. I planned to help my brother reassemble the engine he'd taken apart and left in pieces all over their garage last spring. And for Melissa? Well, all her polliwogs had turned into frogs and hopped away. When I got to Michigan, I would buy her an iguana and all the gear she'd need to raise it.

Although I was vaguely embarrassed, I'd decided to give Walter the portrait that Serenity had painted of me long ago. I couldn't think of anything better. Besides, he was such a sentimental sap — I knew he'd like it.

I planned to stay in Michigan and help Walter at Walkabout during the holiday rush. Then I'd drive back to California, find an apartment in the city, and begin classes at one of the best culinary schools in the country. I figured if I was going to become a famous French chef, I should learn from the experts. My inheritance from Turbo would cover my tuition fees, and a part-time mechanic's job would help with the rest of my expenses. Walter's monthly stipend will fill in the gaps. I'd decided I definitely preferred pastry dough to grease under my fingernails. Who knows, maybe I'd become the next Wolfgang Puck. Or Alice Waters. Maybe I'd even start a new restaurant in Arena Beach one of these days, but I'd open only for dinner so I wouldn't compete with Bill's breakfasts and lunches at the Snack Shack.

What was that? Ghosts? I listened carefully in the shadowy living room but heard nothing more until an onshore breeze rushed across the Bay and up the hill and rattled the roof shingles.

I tucked a key under the geranium on the porch for Curtis and Donald, slid behind the wheel of the Shark, and took one long, final look at the cottage before backing out of the driveway.

I drove past the gas station lot and noticed, beneath the tangle of rain-flattened weeds, patches of tentative green shoots. Smiling, I continued on, past the Sand Bar and the Lip and the fire station. Then I circled around the block and honked good-bye to Bill at the Snack Shack.

Finally I headed up the mountain, feasting on views of the ocean and lagoon as I looped temporarily westward on the switchbacks. On the last wide pull-out, I stopped the Shark and watched a hang glider begin its graceful, descending spiral from the ridge above to the beach below.

The panorama before me looked like the detailed embroidery on my graduation gown, except for one thing. Between the mountain and the beach, running right through the lagoon and up the valley to the north, was a great geologic gash — the San Andreas Fault! All my life I'd lived in Arena Beach, considered it the most peaceful, most beautiful, and safest place on earth and never acknowledged a fact that I'd studied in school and knew in some deep part of myself. Arena Beach sat directly on top of one of the world's major fault lines.

As I stared at that portentous crease in the earth, I had to admit that security was only a dream, an illusion. No place on earth was entirely safe. If an earthquake didn't strike, there were always hurricanes or tornadoes or tsunamis, drunk drivers, psychopathic killers, airplane crashes, AIDS. Life, by its very nature, wasn't predictable or safe. Only death brought guarantees.

234

A person could sit around and worry about potential disasters or simply get on with life.

Lots of people had tried to teach me that lesson in one way or another. Skeg had taught me the importance of facing my fears. Walter had taught me that hurt and pain were as vital a part of life as joy. And Celestial had shown me that living and loving were two very deliberate, powerful, interwoven acts.

What about Turbo? I think my great bear of a friend was afraid of life. His mother had damaged him terribly when he was a kid, and he never recovered. To protect himself from more hurt, he just closed up and got progressively angrier and more bitter until he couldn't stand himself any longer. I wish I could have helped him somehow. Maybe I did. What was his final note to me, if not an act of love?

Even with all these experienced teachers, I never fully understood the power of love until the earthquake, until I heard Julio cry. Suddenly I stopped worrying about the height of the freeway and the darkness of the cavern and the probability of aftershocks. I only knew that I had to find that voice, had to help whoever was crying.

The hang glider I'd been watching leveled out above the beach, lifted slightly, then scooted across the sand, and came to rest. I closed my eyes briefly, sealing the picture in my mind. Even though I was leaving Arena Beach behind, I was taking many precious things with me — all of my childhood memories and growing pains, visions of the beach and the mountain and the ocean, and, of course, Celestial's love.

I shifted the Shark into gear and continued up the mountain road into the trees. At the road's crest I paused. A bobcat streaked across the pavement and vanished beneath the redwoods.

I leaned on the horn and hollered. With the exception of the Sierra and the Rockies, the road was all downhill from here.